Truth is often masked

behind the realm
of good intentions....

Shroud of Silence

CAROL D. SLAMA

BETHANY HOUSE PUBLISHERS
MINNEAPOLIS, MINNESOTA 55438

Shroud of Silence
Copyright © 1998
Carol D. Slama

Cover illustration by William Graf
Cover design by Peter Glöege

Published by Bethany House Publishers
A Ministry of Bethany Fellowship International
11300 Hampshire Avenue South
Minneapolis, Minnesota 55438

Printed in the United States of America by
Bethany Press International, Minneapolis, Minnesota 55438

Library of Congress Cataloging-in-Publication Data

Slama, Carol D.
   Shroud of silence / by Carol D. Slama.
      p.cm. — (Portraits)
    ISBN 0–7642–2039-X (pbk.)
    I. Title. II. Series: Portraits (Minneapolis, Minn.)
PS3569.L257S57   1997
813'.54—dc21   97–33861
                                                  CIP

To Mom and Dad,
who set a great example for
what being a Christian is all about.

And to Brad,
for your support and the humorous postscripts
you sneak on my computer when I'm not looking.
I love you.

Portraits

CAROL D. SLAMA is a first-time author whom Bethany is delighted to introduce under the PORTRAITS line. A graduate of Pacific Lutheran University, Carol has held a number of positions over the years, but her current and most enjoyable job is that of at-home-mom and writer-in-residence. She and her husband have two young sons and make their home in Anchorage, Alaska.

One

Marissa Tomsen looked past the oak table and chairs in her dining room toward the kitchen clock. Ten-thirty. And still no Michael. Pushing aside an assortment of legal papers, insurance claims, and other documents, Marissa walked to the phone and called her brother again. The first message she had left on his answering machine had been a humorous scolding. This one, however, would not be. No matter how much they both despised dealing with these documents, it had to be done. Besides, Michael promised early last week he would come over tonight.

The phone rang half an hour later, and Marissa bit her lip and prayed that they wouldn't have angry words again. She pushed her thick dark hair behind her ear, anticipating Michael's voice. But the caller wasn't Michael. Instead, it was the *Tribune* night manager inquiring why Michael hadn't been to work for three days.

"This is so typical of Michael," Marissa muttered as she grabbed her coat and purse and drove across town to the house he rented. She pulled up beside her brother's familiar four-wheel-drive truck and determinedly walked up the steps to the front door. Michael had probably gone on one of his biking excursions and forgot to tell anyone, although she thought he had outgrown most of his irresponsible impulsiveness when he became a reporter with the *Tribune* a year ago.

She rang the doorbell and then felt around in her purse for the key he'd given her. Something caught her eye and she glanced up. A chill slithering up her spine, she hesitated before inserting the key. Marissa suddenly realized that except for a distant street light, it was pitch black outside. Maybe she shouldn't go in alone. Maybe she should call the police.

"Get a grip," she muttered out loud as she discarded the macabre scenarios that invaded her thoughts, unlocked the door, and pushed it open. Despite her bravery, she probed nervously along the wall until she flipped the switch and light flooded the area. Her eyes darted around the room and then down the hallway.

"Michael?" she called out, her voice shaky and timid. Cautiously, she made her way inside. Michael was tidy but not fastidious, and most times he had things piled here and there. Marissa willed her heart to slow its pace as she surveyed the room. Everything seemed normal.

Then she saw a dark figure moving quickly, silently, down the hall away from her. Frozen, she watched the shadow disappear into the bedroom. A second later Marissa grabbed Michael's baseball bat and turned for the front door. There was a squeak of a window being opened as she ran outside. Halfway down the walk, she heard tires squeal and a car raced out of sight.

Shaking, she leaned her petite body against the cold siding of the house, clutching the baseball bat to her chest. All she could do was pull in deep, steadying breaths, one after the other. What did the intruder want? Where was Michael? She had a sickening feeling that her brother was in trouble—that something was dreadfully wrong. Gripping the bat tighter, she went inside and dialed 9–1–1.

After a vigilant wait by the front window, Marissa saw a Portland Police Department squad car park and two policemen climb out. A wave of unease washed over her when she recognized them. These two had been at the scene of her parents' fatal crash. Sirens, bright lights, yelling, too many people in too tight of an area. Marissa had been stopped along with other people walking downtown that hot summer evening. An ambulance needed to get through, and she had waited and looked over, curious herself.

"A bad one, huh?" she had overheard one of the unneeded, retreating officers say to his partner.

The mustached officer had shrugged as he took a bite of his apple. "Yeah. But they were pretty old anyway."

The thoughtless words had ricocheted through her mind seconds before she recognized her parents' car. They were declared dead at the hospital two hours later.

The doorbell rang. Marissa took a deep breath and forced herself to open it.

"Did you call the police?" the mustached officer asked. Robinson was etched on his brass name tag. Marissa nodded while his partner looked past her into the room. "What's the problem?"

Marissa tried to bury the feelings welling within her, but she found she couldn't—wouldn't—meet their eyes as she ushered them in. "There was someone inside the house when I came in," she began. "When he saw me, he ran down the hall and climbed out the bedroom window. I saw a car speed away but it was too dark to make out the model. The guy looked about five feet ten, had a small build. He was wearing all black."

"Did this person hurt you?" the younger officer asked.

"No."

"Did he take anything?"

"I don't know. This is my brother's place. I came over because I was worried about him. His boss said he hasn't been to work for three days, and that isn't like Michael. I mean, he likes his job, and he goes to the gym faithfully three times a week. Overall he's a really—" she paused, realizing she was rambling.

"Can we look around?" Robinson asked.

Marissa nodded, frustrated that her emotions were preventing her from communicating effectively.

After searching the house and asking another series of questions, the younger officer looked over the notes he had taken and said, "So you don't live here?"

"No," Marissa said, hoping that fact wasn't going to stop their investigation.

"We didn't see any signs of forced entry," Robinson said. "Who else has a key to the house?"

"Just my brother and me."

"Are you sure?"

Marissa's gaze faltered. She wasn't sure.

The officers exchanged a knowing look. "I'll run a criminal history," the younger officer said as he walked out the door toward the squad car.

There was a long pause before Robinson stopped jotting notes in his book and turned his attention back to Marissa. "Does your brother do drugs? Gamble?" he asked.

"No," Marissa said quickly.

"Do you know many of his friends?"

"Yes, most of them. They are nice, upstanding guys." She knew what he was getting at, and her irritation flared. Her brother was not a lawbreaker.

"Officer Bennett is pulling up some information on Michael. It's standard procedure for situations like this—nothing to get alarmed about."

"Nothing to get alarmed about?" she said impatiently. "My brother is missing. I think I'm alarmed." A mix of raw nerves and fear of the unknown was causing sarcasm to punctuate her words. "Can you help me find my brother or not?"

"We can try, but first we need to determine whether he is truly missing. Why don't you begin by checking with family and friends," Robinson said with fluid ease, attempting to calm Marissa's agitation. "If you still can't locate him, then come down to the station and file a missing persons report."

"Negative on criminal," Bennett informed as he walked back inside.

Robinson nodded and looked back to Marissa. "I'm going to be candid with you. We've done as much as we can tonight.

Tomorrow when we're back on shift again, we'll canvas the area—talk to the neighbors, see if they saw anything suspicious or if they saw the intruder. Then we'll do a follow-up with you, write a report, and depending on what we find, this case could very well be suspended. I'm sorry, there's just not much to go on. Of course, you can file that missing persons report. We do take those seriously."

Marissa nodded—not in agreement, but in understanding that they were giving up. She would file the report, but she had little confidence that an already overloaded system could help her.

After the police departed, she looked the room over, trying not to give in to feelings of frustration and despair. It was too late to call any of Michael's friends, and as for family—well, Marissa *was* family for Michael, since their parents' deaths. Determined to get some answers, she locked the dead bolt, turned on every light in the house, and began a search of her own. There must be something that might provide a clue to Michael's whereabouts.

Marissa began to mentally take inventory of what she saw. There was no sign of a struggle, and Michael's stereo and TV remained, ruling out burglary. A backpack tossed in the corner entryway produced nothing significant, and neither did the loose mail next to it. Several coats hung in the hall closet, and a couple pairs of sweat pants lay on the floor. All she found in the pockets were gum wrappers, grocery receipts, and coins.

Inspecting the kitchen, Marissa opened the refrigerator. A half-eaten pizza—Michael's favorite dinner—and a few other foods with old expiration dates took up only a fraction of the shelf space. It really didn't look any different from normal. Michael generally ate out.

Several dresser drawers in the bedroom were ajar, but the clothes inside appeared to be in order. His closet seemed normal, and Marissa recognized the large suitcase he had taken back and forth to college on the top shelf.

A postcard lay on his nightstand. Marissa turned it over, read the short, innocuous note from Lauren, then noted the date—nine months ago. He'd had a difficult time over their breakup. Lauren was a journalist, too, and they had dated for nearly a year. But Lauren put her career before romance, and when she was offered a job in Los Angeles, she left with barely more than a good-bye. Michael had been devastated. He'd hardly dated since, and Marissa could tell he hadn't completely gotten over her.

As Marissa neared the foot of the bed, she nearly stumbled over a stack of sports magazines. A notebook lay beside them. She picked up the hardbound notebook and found Bible study handouts inside. Scanning the pages, she noticed Michael had answered questions every day for what looked like several weeks. He'd never attended adult Sunday school at their home church, much less one that assigned homework. Maybe she had been wrong about New Covenant, the church he'd been attending. She set the notebook down and restacked the magazines.

In the spare bedroom, Michael's rolltop desk was in its usual messy state. She pressed the "play" button on his answering machine as she scanned the many notes and messages strewn across his desk. She waited, but nothing happened. Thinking she hadn't pressed the button hard enough, she tried a second time. Still nothing. Finally, she opened the top. Both tapes were missing.

A slight shudder went through Marissa, for she'd heard the recording just before she came over. The intruder's silhouette sprang to her memory. Suddenly the room seemed darker than the rest of the house. He had been in this very room. He must have taken the tapes. She quickly walked back to the living room, her heart pounding. What message had been important enough for someone to break in and take? She considered the policemen's inquiries about Michael's involvement in drugs or gambling, but then she shook her head. There was no basis, no evidence.

Marissa glanced at a stack of CDs on the floor and then picked up a baseball mitt from the coffee table. Memories of having to sort through her parents' things after their funeral flooded her mind. She swallowed hard. "Michael's not dead," she told herself resolutely. "He left on a bike trip and there was a petty thief in the house. That's all."

It had been only eight months since their parents died from the auto accident. Both Marissa and Michael had been badly shaken at the time. Marissa lived through the first month in a foggy, numbed state, even through the processing of the will and other legal documents their uncle Hiram, executor of the will, had given them. Every paper they had to sign seemed futile. What they wanted more than anything material was to have their parents back with them.

Marissa silently dealt with her pain at the funeral, then cried out loud about God's justice for nights afterward. Life didn't seem fair. And Michael's staying in the denial stage for months hadn't been easy on anybody—himself included.

Blinking away tears, Marissa set down the mitt and walked to the stereo cabinet, where she picked up a framed photo of her and Michael. They were standing in front of their parents' home, only months before the accident. Michael's six-foot frame towered over hers, and his light brown hair looked wind-blown. He was wearing sweats and a T-shirt and stood straddling his racing bike.

It was almost too much to bear, seeing his familiar crooked smile. The same fear washed over her as when Michael had been seven and had gotten lost at the state fair. She had been responsible for him. It had been her fault.

"We asked you to watch him while we got the hot dogs!" her father had erupted. Marissa's mouth quivered from shame and fear, and tears streamed down her cheeks.

"No time to scold," she remembered her mother saying. *"Let's just find him."*

"I need to find you," Marissa whispered, clutching the frame to her. "God, please tell me what to do. You know where Michael is. You know if he's in trouble or if he's been injured. Please help me, Lord—I feel so alone. And I miss Mom and Dad so much. . . ." The rest of her prayer was jumbled as she wrestled with feelings of wanting to lean on Jesus, while at the same time wanting to accuse Him of causing her pain and fear. Despite her yearning to know God's comfort, anger and self-pity seemed her strongest emotions.

Marissa's temples throbbed with a dull headache as she wiped her eyes and moved to replace the picture. Then she hesitated. There on the speaker, behind where the picture had been, was a pendant. She picked up the golden, oval piece of jewelry and studied the etching. A dragon's head framed by a rainbow. Michael didn't wear jewelry, and she thought it odd that he would own such a piece. Or maybe it was a friend's. But why would a friend put something behind a picture frame? Why would Michael?

The sound of a car driving slowly down the alley behind the house unsettled her, and she waited, listening warily until it passed by. Suddenly Marissa possessed an undeniable urge to leave. She slipped the pendant into her pocket and forced herself back to the spare bedroom, where she quickly scooped up the miscellaneous papers from Michael's desk and shoved them in a shopping bag. She grabbed her coat and was about to unlock the front door when she noticed a piece of paper half-hidden underneath the couch. Why such a small thing caught her eye, she didn't know. Anxious to leave, but curious, too, she set the bag down and hurried across the room. It was a note to her in Michael's handwriting—two sentences that didn't make sense. She stuffed the paper in the bag, made an anxious dash to her car, and was relieved when she arrived home twenty minutes later.

After a few hours of fitful sleep, Marissa padded into the kitchen. Her well-established ritual of grinding fresh coffee beans for her morning cup and reading from her Bible was thwarted. The coffee ended up too strong, and her mind refused to think of anything other than Michael. She called her boss's secretary and told her that she wouldn't be in until ten. Dedication and a special talent for writing original and well-accepted copy had earned her a level of autonomy at Jonah Stevens Advertising Agency.

Tired yet restless, she looked down at the bag full of papers and retrieved the note she'd found near Michael's couch. Maybe now, after some sleep, the words would make sense. But still they didn't. Marissa shook her head in frustration. Nothing was making sense. Unless . . . no, it was a crazy thought. She took another sip of the potent coffee and looked out at the early morning sun shining on a patch of dew-laden azaleas in the backyard. But the thought held fast. She continued to stare, recalling a memory of fifteen years before. . . .

"Don't run so fast. I can't keep up." Twelve-year-old Marissa was breathless when she caught up with eleven-year-old Michael, finally stationary in the tree house.

"What's so important?"

"A code." Michael said the words softly, as if the walls truly did have ears.

"A what?"

"I've named it the code of silence. But before I tell you how it works, you have to promise that you'll never tell anyone else. Ever."

Marissa looked into her brother's eyes. He was terribly serious, and she knew that if she didn't play along he'd be disappointed. Anyway, it sounded kind of exciting so she promised.

"It goes like this," Michael began, his sandy brown cowlick standing up like an antenna. "I say, like, tell your best friend Ramona that—"

"But my best friend isn't Ramona."

"I know. That's part of the code. Just wait until I'm done and you'll understand." Marissa sighed and listened as her brother continued. "Anyway, tell Ramona that I'm not going to be ready at two o'clock so go alone to the dance." Michael looked pleased with himself, and Marissa looked at him expectantly.

"So? What does it mean?"

"Anything I say that doesn't make sense, use the first letter. Any number I say use as a vowel, like *A* is one, *E* is two, *I* is three, *O* is four, and *U* is five," he explained, counting off on his fingers. "Now try to figure it out."

Marissa sighed and rolled her eyes. He was the whiz in English, not her. "The first letter is *R*, 'cause we don't even know a Ramona, the next is *E* for two o'clock, and last one's *D* 'cause you wouldn't be caught dead dancing."

"So what does it spell?" Michael asked, his eyes bright and eager.

"R-E-D. Red."

"Right! Think of it. We could say one thing and mean another. Isn't it great?"

Marissa didn't think so at the outset, but over the course of the summer, they found countless uses for the code. Not only could they communicate privately at the dinner table without their parents understanding, they could outwit their friends, too.

The neighborhood kids were eager to learn the code and begged for them to share it, but the brother and sister solemnly kept their pact.

Marissa looked back to the note, at first chastising herself for thinking like a twelve-year-old again. It had only been a silly childhood code. But here was a note from Michael containing a couple of sentences that didn't make sense. Marissa hesitated as she reached for a pencil and piece of paper. Could a childhood game be the key to understanding the strange events of the past day? She read the note again.

Marissa,
    Feed Henry, there's only two cans of food left. Liver and Presto.

                     Mike.

Check my mail #153.

Michael didn't own a pet. He was always Michael and hated anyone calling him Mike. The last line didn't make sense, either, as he didn't have a post office box.

She wrote the first letter, *H*. Then *E*, and then the other letters. H-E-L-P-M-A-U-I. Was this just a joke he was playing on her?

The next day, when she discovered her savings account had been emptied, she thought not.

Two

W hat do you mean, my account won't cover this?" Marissa said with a look of disbelief after the bank teller denied her a withdrawal of two hundred dollars. The prospect of insufficient funds was absurd. She had left her inheritance money in the savings account until she could decide where to invest it. "You must be mistaken. I have over one hundred thousand dollars in there."

"You opened the account six months ago," the bank teller told her in a low voice as he eyed the computer screen. "It's a joint account. Your cosigner, a Michael G. Tomsen, withdrew the money a few days ago."

Color drained from Marissa's face and she found it hard to swallow. She held on to the cold marble countertop, steadying herself as if she'd been dealt a physical blow. Michael had done what? She stared at the teller, feeling the first ripples of queasiness in her stomach.

"He withdrew all of it?" she questioned, her voice a strangled whisper.

"Yes. Four days ago." The teller avoided eye contact as he rechecked the computer monitor. "Would you like a copy of the withdrawal slip?"

She nodded woodenly, and he disappeared around the corner. Numb and yet cognizant enough to feel the curious stares of those around her, she endured the wait, attempting to regain her composure. She looked up at the familiar painting of an Oregonian pioneer family. That same picture had probably been on the wall when she and Michael first opened accounts there fifteen years ago. What had they been saving for? Bicycles? She took a deep breath, flinching at thoughts of her brother's betrayal. Had Michael delved into something illegal as the police suggested?

The teller returned and slid the withdrawal slip toward Marissa's trembling fingers. Marissa looked at the document in deafening silence as her expression changed from disbelief to recognition to incredible discomfort. Either Michael had signed the withdrawal himself, or a practiced forger had.

Marissa found it difficult to think and struggled with what to do next. After a moment the teller, obviously anxious to help others, looked beyond her at the line of waiting customers and then back to her. There was nothing to say, apparently nothing more to do. In dejection she picked up the slip of paper and left.

Driving home in the pouring rain, she tried to make sense of what was happening. Michael and the money . . . gone. Together? Separate? Was he having financial struggles? Did he have enemies? He certainly wouldn't have a job at the *Tribune* if he stayed away any longer, and he had worked so hard to get the position. Why would he do this to himself? To her? Suddenly she felt as though she hardly knew Michael. The thought was foreign, frightening, even strangely ominous. Could it be that Michael had been hiding things from her?

Yesterday Marissa had called every number Michael had jotted down on the inside cover of his phone book. Lauren first. She acted somewhat surprised over the phone call and said she had no idea where he might be. When Lauren's reporter skills kicked in and she began asking investigative questions, Marissa politely ended the conversation. Michael's other friends didn't have a clue.

Her call to New Covenant seemed more positive. "He's missing?" the elderly woman's voice said over the phone. "Michael Tomsen? Why, he's such a nice young man. I see him here often. He comes to church every Sunday and is involved in one of our Bible courses." She sounded genuinely concerned. "Let me check the attendance chart on the computer and see when he was last in church."

Marissa heard keys clicking on a computer keyboard as she waited.

"He hasn't been to church or the Bible course in two weeks," the woman said. She paused. "I'm ashamed that I didn't personally notice. This church is just too big, and it's hard to keep track of everyone. I'm sorry." This woman was the first person who had taken Marissa seriously. And when the woman offered to take her name and number and personally pray for her—as well as put her concern on the church's prayer chain—Marissa was encouraged.

Afterward, she thought of her own church. The prayer chain was without a chairman and essentially not functioning. She tried calling the pastor, but he was away at a conference. And while the assistant pastor talked with her, she had the feeling that he considered her situation contrived. Why was it that Michael's church—one that she considered an odd denomination—held the warmth?

Marissa continued to feel overwhelmed as she pulled into her driveway. Her parents were gone and now Michael. Even the church she had attended since childhood seemed not to be what she had always thought. What was happening to her once-secure world?

Anxiety rested heavy on her shoulders. Not caring that it was still pouring down rain, she made her ritual trip to the mailbox at the end of the driveway, hoping to find something—anything—from Michael. Junk mail and two bills. She turned back toward the house, crying in little hiccups, the unknowns burying her in worry and despair. A moment later her shoe landed on a slug and she slid erratically. Mail flew from her hands as she tried to regain her balance, but despite her efforts, she fell hard on the cold, muddy concrete steps. Her head spun crazily, as much from her emotions as from the tumble she had just taken.

Attempting to get up, her vision blurred as scattered thoughts whirled through her head. Everything was changing so fast; everyone she loved was gone. For the first time in her life she didn't care about tomorrow—much less the mud on her suit. Life had turned as cold and unrelenting as the concrete she lay on. She quit trying to get up as stars turned to blackness and she sank back into a crumpled heap, her tears intermingling with the rain.

❧ ❧ ❧ ❧

Marissa woke to the soft sounds of praise music as she lay on Myrtle and Ernest Thibedeaux's couch. The dimly lit living room, cozy and familiar, slowly came into focus.

"How do you feel, honey?" a concerned voice asked, and soon Myrtle's warm countenance filled Marissa's view.

"Like I've been beat up," Marissa said, licking her dry lips and smiling cautiously at her elderly neighbor. She slowly caressed the homemade quilt covering her.

"You had us worried," Myrtle said, concern in her eyes. "You must have fallen on the steps. Ernest wants to take a look at your eyes—check for a concussion. He may be retired, but he'll always be a doctor."

"Sounds like a good idea," Marissa said, moving stiffly until she sat upright on the couch. "I think I saw stars."

Deep-set eyes, thinning gray hair, and once built like a rock, Ernest walked in a few minutes later and set his black medical bag down next to Marissa. "Snoozing on the steps can be pretty uncomfortable," he said with a twinkle in his eyes.

Marissa smiled and accepted the thermometer he slid under her tongue.

After checking her eyes and reflexes with practiced motions, he read the thermometer. "You're okay," he said. "But you're going to get a phone call from me at about three A.M. to make sure you're not a candidate for a coma." He patted her leg and stood. When he did, the joints in his knees made a cracking sound. "I'll bet both you gals can diagnose that sound," he said with a chuckle as he joined his wife on the couch. "It's called old age."

"Thanks, you two," Marissa said, appreciative of her neighbors who had acted like parents to her even before she had lost her own. "I don't know what I'd do without you." Ernest and Myrtle were genuine Christians, filled with faith, love, and enthusiasm. They prayed and cared for her as if she were their own daughter, and they thought the world of Michael.

Michael. Marissa knew the thought of him in some kind of danger would worry them, but she felt they deserved to know the truth. And she desperately needed to share her burden in the warmth of their acceptance.

"But where would he go?" Myrtle asked after Marissa told them about Michael's disappearance and the missing money. "And why wouldn't he tell one of us?" Her voice was painfully uneasy.

"Doesn't sound like Michael," Ernest said. "At least not since he started working at the *Tribune*."

"I know," Marissa said, realizing that he, too, had noticed a maturing in Michael this past year.

Ernest gazed thoughtfully toward the fireplace, then looked back to Marissa. His many years of doctoring provided him a calm, and yet Marissa sensed the depth of his worry. "Both his truck and bike were at the house?"

Marissa nodded.

"Was he having problems at work?"

"I don't think so," Marissa said. "I've talked with his boss and called most all his friends. Even Lauren. None of them has any idea where he could be. I filed a missing persons report with the police, gave them his picture, and called and called regarding what I should do. I even searched his house myself. Nothing adds up." She paused. "Except maybe a note."

"He left a note?" Myrtle said.

"I think so," Marissa said, squeezing her hands together in her lap. "I know it sounds strange, but he and I had a code when we were kids. If I translate the note with our code, I'm able to spell out the words 'Help Maui.' All I can think about is that he's in some kind of trouble in Hawaii." She paused, realizing how absurd the note sounded and yet feeling terribly swayed by her instincts to protect her brother. Finally, she voiced what was forefront in her thoughts. "I want to go to Maui and try to find him."

A silence hung as heavy as the tapestry curtains that adorned the walls nearby until Myrtle stood. "Ernest," she said, motioning for him to follow her into the kitchen. Marissa heard the exchange of their low voices and then Ernest calling someone on the phone. Several minutes later, they walked back in the living room.

Myrtle sat down on the couch and put her wrinkled hand tenderly over Marissa's. "We're as worried about Michael as you are. If you think he's in Maui, then go. We called our friends who own the condominium we stay in when we go over there. They don't have renters lined up for the next two months. After we explained your situation, they offered to let you stay there for next to nothing."

"We have only one request," Ernest added. "Hire a professional investigator, Marissa. We don't want you in any danger."

Marissa nodded and a smile flitted across her face—the first time in what seemed like weeks. Their approval confirmed her decision to go.

"We'll be praying for you," Myrtle said, giving her a heartfelt hug.

☙ ☙ ❧ ❧

Two days later, after making arrangements to leave work, Marissa flew to Maui and hired a private investigator. After a week of bills and no information, she hired another P.I. but soon learned that he liked to drink his lunches and dinners on a barstool. She dismissed him, too.

Her finances were dwindling. She had to continue making

house and car payments back home, and her vacation pay would soon run out. Her checking account miserably low, Marissa knew she had to find some source of income. Left with no other options, she opened the classified section of the newspaper.

Three

Marissa wiped the back of her hand across her forehead, not yet acclimated to the heavy, tropical air that enveloped her. This wasn't at all like Portland. No, Maui had become an in-between world for her, a no-man's land.

Marissa walked to the spacious condominium's bedroom and put on her newly acquired uniform, trying not to notice the pilled cotton of the fitted print dress. She smoothed the collar as though it were one of her wool gabardine suits, but instead of picking up a leather attaché, she slipped a slim wallet in her pocket and walked four blocks to the Regency Hotel. She wanted to be on time for her training as hostess in the main dining room.

Her college degree had no place here. John Stiles, the restaurant night manager, had selected her on looks alone. He'd even told her so when he'd hired her, his eyes taking notice of her slim body and thick dark hair throughout the interview.

In any other situation, she would have walked away and not looked back. But she needed the job, and John had been agreeable to part-time evening hours, a schedule four other restaurants hadn't been willing to offer.

She walked through the elegant hotel foyer full of lush tropical greenery to the elevator lobby and pushed the up arrow. A handsome couple waited nearby.

"I hope your parents won't be late this time, Sheila," the man said, obviously agitated.

The woman tossed her long blond hair back and looped her arm possessively through his. "Don't worry, Spencer," she said, tempering his eyes with hers. "Next time I'll say no."

"You said that the last time they invited themselves," Spencer said, his voice deliberately low.

A large-boned woman wearing a Polynesian print dress and a man, slightly shorter and nearly bald, appeared.

"Hello, Mother. Hi, Daddy," Sheila said, turning toward them.

"Sheila, you look beautiful—as usual," the mother said, reaching to give her daughter a kiss on the cheek as expensive jewelry collided and spun on her arm. "Hello, Spencer," she said morosely, pursing her lips as if the words tasted bad in her mouth. The father gave his daughter a quick hug and shook Spencer's hand.

When the elevator door opened, Marissa caught the mother's condescending look—as if hotel employees shouldn't be allowed to ride the same elevator as guests. Marissa looked down and fidgeted with her necklace, desiring to wait for another car. But a moment later she glanced up and saw Spencer holding the door for her. She hesitated, but then thanked him with a small smile and walked on, edging to the back. One short elevator ride couldn't be that torturous, she thought.

Marissa alternated glances between the quickly changing floor numbers and the back of Sheila's neck, wondering if her diamond studded necklace and earrings were real. Suddenly there was a jolt and the elevator stopped. The panel overhead went blank, and the doors remained pressed tightly together. A look of restlessness crept to each of their faces—all except the mother. She seemed irritated.

Spencer was quick to take charge. He pushed the down button several times, and when nothing happened, he tried several others. The elevator remained inert. "This is a first for these elevators," he said, bending down to open the knee-high panel for the emergency phone. "They've never stuck before." Spencer's comment bordered between a brave apology and uneasiness. Marissa wondered if he worked for the hotel.

"Oh great," Spencer sighed, more upset than anything as he held the receiver. "The phone line's been cut."

"Probably those juvenile delinquents you hired to clean the pool," the older woman commented dryly.

"Isn't there anything we can do?" the father asked, his voice small and tight. "We're at least ten floors in the air, you know."

"It's probably just a power outage," Spencer said, running his fingers through his dark, thick hair. "These elevators stop and lock when power's cut off."

"It can't be a power outage," the mother interjected, annoyance pulling heavily on her powder-pressed wrinkles. "The lights in here are still on."

"They could be on backup generators," Spencer said, pushing more buttons. He seemed tense, and Sheila's mother appeared to be the cause. Marissa couldn't imagine having to cope with her tiresome questions and sarcasm for an entire evening. Marissa wondered why he put up with the agitation. Of course, Sheila *was* a beauty.

"Someone in your position should *know* what's going on," the older woman continued.

"Mother," Sheila said, noticeably ruffled. "Spencer can't have an answer for everything."

Marissa looked at her watch, seeing the time she was to train before her shift flutter by. She sighed. This was certainly not the way she wanted to begin her new job, but there was nothing she could do. She would simply have to wait out the mechanical malfunction and endure the accompanying bickering.

At a scuffling sound heard overhead, all five pairs of eyes looked up. A drill whined, and then a vent in the roof moved. Spencer appeared relieved and said, "Sounds like a maintenance man fixing the problem."

"If we're expected to climb out of this thing, I refuse," the older woman balked.

Spencer looked expectantly toward the opening. "Hey, up there. Can you tell us what's wrong?"

"Nothing's wrong," a sinister voice said. "Now just shut up."

Spencer stiffened, and Sheila clutched his arm, looking horrified. Marissa's heart rate doubled as she pressed her back against the padded wall, feeling like a trapped animal. A moment later a crude-looking cloth bag tied to a stick was lowered through the opening.

"Put your money and jewelry in the bag. I have a gun and a clear view, so don't hold anything back."

The mother lost all composure and began sobbing. The father held her arm tightly, trembling himself.

"You first," the voice said as the bag dropped directly in front of the hysterical woman.

The father helped remove his wife's jewelry, then unclenched her fingers from around her eel skin satchel. He dropped everything into the bag, including his own wallet, and grasped his wife's arm again. "That's all we have," he said, his voice unnaturally high.

The cloth bag floated to Spencer, who forfeited his Rolex watch and wallet. With a look of sheer horror, Sheila removed her diamond necklace, earrings, and a pearl ring, and dropped them and her clutch in the bag, then buried her face in Spencer's lapel.

Marissa was already unclasping the pendant when it was her turn. She deposited only her ring, watch, and thin coin purse, then waited for a bullet to come searing though her chest because of her small token. But instead of a bullet, she felt the fabric of the bag brush against her hair as it was lifted back up through the hole.

"Aloha," the voice said with dripping sarcasm. More scuffling sounds, then all was quiet.

The older man comforted his wife, who looked dreadfully white.

"He's gone," Spencer said with relief. "Is everyone okay?"

Sheila looked up with wide, frightened eyes and then turned back toward Spencer's shoulder as if he would shield her from further disaster.

Marissa nodded, silently wishing she had a pair of arms holding her, too. Adrenaline pumped vigorously through her body, but surprisingly, the fear she had felt disappeared with the thief. Was it courage from God that uplifted her, or was it that she felt she had nothing more to lose?

Ten long minutes went by before the elevator came to life. After a small jerk, it made a gradual descent, and the doors opened to the lobby, humming with its usual activity. No one seemed to have noticed or cared that one of the elevators had remained between floors for so long. The robbery had been a success, and no doubt the robber was far from the area by now.

"Could you all wait over there?" Spencer said, motioning to a corner couch. "I'll be right back." Marissa sat down stiffly, watching as Spencer walked behind the front desk and talked in a low voice to a uniformed clerk. He acted very much in command and returned a few minutes later. "Plainclothes policemen are on their way," Spencer said. "Each of us will need to fill out a report. It shouldn't take long."

"You expect me to fill out a report?" Sheila's mother shrilled. "I don't want to write now any more than I want to eat one more meal in this stuffy hotel."

Spencer ignored her comment and walked back behind the desk. Sheila and her father sat silent and stone faced.

Marissa looked away from the family threesome. She had no desire to wait or to fill out a police report. Her watch was replaceable, her coin purse held only a few dollars, and she should have gotten rid of the meaningless ring from Donald months ago. Most important, the pendant was safe. Unbeknownst to the thief and the others in the elevator, she had undone the clasp and let it slide down her blouse. No. Something more than this would have to happen before she dealt with the police again.

With Spencer preoccupied, Marissa mumbled that she needed to use the restroom. She walked to the far end of the foyer, slipped back into the elevator lobby, and endured the ride up to the restaurant.

"Sorry I'm late," Marissa told the waiting hostess. "I was—"

"Forget the excuses," the young woman said hotly, handing Marissa a piece of paper. "My boyfriend's waiting. Here, memorize tonight's specials." A moment later she disappeared behind an "employees only" door.

Marissa read the paper briefly and then smiled hesitantly at the elderly couple approaching the podium.

"Welcome," she said, fumbling for two menus. "I mean . . . Aloha."

Four

*M*ichael tried to block out the sound of the man speaking endlessly in the front of the room. What did they want from him? Would he dare to bolt through the row of desks and make a move for the door? He glanced behind him and thought not. Derrick, the hulk, was sitting nearby, trying to blend in as a class participant and not the bodyguard he really was. This was nothing short of insanity. Tourists wearing T-shirts and shorts walked just outside the window. Children laughed loudly, playing in a nearby park. But he was being held against his will.

The chair felt hard to him, and he squirmed. The motel they had him in was cheap and dirty, and he wasn't used to sleeping on such a thin mattress. Michael hadn't been allowed to exercise at all in the four days he'd been held, and he thought about how hard it would be to train all over again.

Michael felt horrible about lying to Marissa. He and his sister had always been close—well, except for the past seven months when she had fallen hard for Donald. But his irritation at Marissa's preoccupation with the suave art director was no excuse for what he had allowed to happen. How had his thinking become so twisted?

Just last month, he felt good about the way his life was turning around. His friends at New Covenant had stepped right in to help him after his parents' death. They'd gotten him to attend church on Sunday mornings—a habit he had fallen out of—and a Bible class that had strict requirements for attendance and preparation. He'd been thankful for the regimen.

He'd even begun attending a self-improvement course. He'd been reluctant at first, knowing the two classes would consume every weekday evening and some weekends. But so many of the people at New Covenant were going that he felt compelled. Besides, the course was only eight weeks long. . . .

After six weeks of faithful attendance, he came down with the flu. Lying in bed, his body aching, Michael looked toward the wall and then down to a stack of sports magazines. They were dusty. His brow furrowed as he stared at the athlete on the cover, and as if he had been awakened from a long sleep, he realized that he hadn't signed up for his favorite triathlon or seen his long-time buddies in weeks. He hadn't even written Lauren—no matter how useless the action would be. Somehow, thinking about all the things he put aside to attend New Covenant made him feel unsettled. But why? Wasn't he becoming closer to God? Striving for personal growth in all areas of his life?

He stared up at the Bible Marissa had given him for Christmas, unused on the bookshelf. Hand-outs were easier, his prayer partner, Ray, had explained. No one would be embarrassed trying to find a verse in the Bible, and they wouldn't have to contend with different translations. Michael knew something was wrong with the concept, but he felt too miserable to think about it and rolled over for the umpteenth time.

An hour later the phone's shrill ring startled him awake. He let it ring twice before moving. "Hello," he said groggily.

"I didn't mean to wake you," the familiar voice said. Michael sighed. It was Ray. He'd called yesterday, interrupting his sleep then, too.

"What's up?" Michael said.

"Just wondering if you needed anything—other than my prayers."

"Yeah. Some sleep."

Ray laughed. "All right. Hope you can make it to class tomorrow night."

"We'll see."

The next day, Michael made it to work but ended up feeling miserable and went home early. He walked straight into the bedroom and collapsed, exhausted. Just as he was dozing off, the phone rang. Thinking it was his alternate at the *Tribune*, he answered. When he heard Ray's voice, something in him snapped.

"You don't need to call me every day," Michael said tersely. "You're bugging me, man."

"Sorry. I'm just concerned about your attendance. You know the rules. Four missed classes and you have to begin all over again."

"I can't plan how long I'm going to be sick."

"I thought you were committed, like the rest of us."

Ray's words angered Michael and he bolted upright. "If you don't call racing to church every night after the gym committed, I don't know what is." He hunched over and put his hand to his head, which pounded from getting up too quickly. "Right now I'm sick. I can't go anywhere."

"The program suggests priorities so you don't fall into the trap of putting work before God—like you did today."

"I had a deadline. I'd like to keep my job."

"But whatever you put first in your—"

"How did you know I went to work?" Michael interrupted, trying to ignore a wave of nausea.

"I . . . I just guessed." Ray never stammered. An alarm went off in Michael's head.

"I'm quitting the class," Michael said, his words terse and even.

"You're struggling, Michael. You sound angry and upset. We care about you and don't want you to disappoint yourself. Why don't you try the meditation exercises? They'll help relieve your tension."

Michael remembered the exercises, the theories, the

PORTRAITS

"truths." "No," he spat out, suddenly convinced that the class was a waste of time.

"But you signed the personal contract. Don't let yourself down."

"I'm not letting myself down and don't call me again!" Michael slammed the phone down and jerked the cord from the wall. Then he paused and reattached the cord. He promised his alternate at the *Tribune* he would be available. Opening the drawer in his nightstand, he pulled out the shrill whistle for prank callers he had planned to give Lauren. "Call back now, Ray," he muttered.

Michael walked to the kitchen, opened the refrigerator, and grabbed a carton of yogurt and a Pepsi. One minute he felt like throwing up, the next he was hungry. He'd probably regret eating, but at the moment he didn't care.

An hour later there was a knock at the door. *Probably Marissa*, he thought to himself. He might as well apologize for his behavior as of late—that would be one monkey off his back. Never hearing from Ray again would be another.

But the caller wasn't his sister, and the two men standing in his doorway didn't look like they were there to tell him he was a sweepstakes winner. One was built like a brick wall, with a pocked face and a large nose. The other was shorter, with impeccably styled hair so blond it almost looked white, and his eyes were pale green and small.

"Michael Tomsen?" the blonde asked.

Michael's heartbeat quickened, immediately sensing something wasn't right. He tried shutting the door, but the larger man's shoulder opposed the force. "We need to talk," the smaller man said. "It's for the best." The powerful figure moved just enough to allow his partner inside.

"If this is about the program," Michael said, "I'm out."

"My name is Lee," the blonde said, holding out his hand. He smiled, but his eyes remained glacial.

Michael denied him a handshake.

After the bruiser let himself in and sentinelled by the door,

Lee's counterfeit politeness disappeared and he laid his briefcase on a nearby coffee table, snapped it open, and took out several documents. "I believe you signed these," he said pointedly.

Michael glanced at the paper work and sighed. "I signed up for a class, that's all."

"We don't offer 'just classes.' You signed papers committing yourself to a program," Lee said.

"Well, now I'm uncommitting myself," Michael said sarcastically. "What is it with you people? Don't you understand anything?"

Lee's expression hardened. "I believe you're the one who doesn't understand." He pulled another document from his case. "We also need the final installation on this."

Michael glanced at the paper, disbelief in his eyes. "How did you get your hands on that?"

"You made an investment, remember?"

"Not with you."

"I guess you didn't read the fine print. You owe us quite a bit."

Michael's hands started to sweat and his stomach turned sour. The class was connected with the investment company Ekvar? Something wasn't right. "I'll have my lawyer call you," Michael said, his voice hard. "Now leave."

"That's exactly what we're going to do," Lee said. He clicked his briefcase shut and motioned toward his partner. "Derrick, why don't you help him pack a carryon. I need to make a call."

"I'm not going anywhere with you guys," Michael said, taking a step back.

"Mr. Tomsen," Lee said, "you can make this as pleasant or uncomfortable as you want. But I guarantee you, you will be coming with us."

The airline tickets Michael had seen in Lee's briefcase were now a terrifying thought. "Okay," Michael blurted, "I'll forfeit the money I've already put in. I just want out."

"A promise is a promise," Lee said, and a second later he walked out the door.

Michael couldn't comprehend what was happening. He was being told—forced—to go with these scam artists? "This is ridiculous," he shouted at the closed door. He was calling the police! But as he turned to walk toward the phone, Derrick pulled out what looked to be a .38 from under his suit jacket. Michael stopped and stared at Derrick as his anger spiraled into fear. These men were not fooling.

"Get your stuff," Derrick commanded, his gun still sighted on Michael's chest.

Realizing he had little choice but to obey, Michael motioned stiffly toward the hall saying, "It's in the bedroom." Derrick nodded and followed him.

Pulling a duffel bag from the top shelf of his closet, Michael looked over at the hulking giant leaning against the door frame, one hand resting on the gun he had slipped back in the holster. All the gallant escapes he'd seen in the movies suddenly seemed terrifying and ridiculously simplistic . . . possible only with stunt men and cooperative villains. He tried to calculate how many precious seconds it would take to dive in the bathroom, lock the door, and climb out the window. All he could visualize were bullets piercing the door and then his back.

He felt helpless without a weapon, and yet he did have something. He knew the power of words—after all, he was a journalist. Words stopped and started wars. Perhaps a few well-phrased questions could provide him with something equal to metal and brawn. He'd already surmised they were flying somewhere. Now to find out where.

"Should I pack sweaters or T-shirts?" Michael asked as he tossed socks and underwear into the open bag. His hands were shaking, but thankfully, his voice sounded calm. Derrick didn't answer. "Look," Michael continued, "half the places in the world are hot, the other half are cold. You won't be giving much away if you just say hot or cold."

Silence.

Michael wasn't about to give up on what could be the most important interview of his life. "Don't tell me that short little geek won't let you talk," Michael taunted.

"Shut up," Derrick spat out.

Bingo. He'd struck a nerve.

"Guess I was right," Michael continued. "He's the brains, you're the brawn. They must not let you in on anything—not even the weather."

Michael expected the look of indignation on Derrick's face, but he didn't know what the emotion would provide. He only hoped pride would overrule prescripts. A moment later Derrick took a step into the room and kicked at a T-shirt crumpled up near the clothes hamper and growled, "You missed."

"Great," Michael said optimistically, opening a bureau drawer. "T-shirts it will be."

Pulling out shorts and a couple polo shirts, Michael's mind worked overtime. They were taking him somewhere warm. Where did the Ekvar presenters say they had programs set up? Where was their main office? In his mind he pictured beaches, but there were beaches lots of places. It was somewhere vacationers go. *Think, think,* he commanded his brain. Mexico, no. Caribbean, no. Hawaii . . . Maui. Was that it?

"Don't worry, I'm almost done," Michael said, glancing up at the tightly fibered man. "Hey, you haven't shot anyone for not packing fast enough, have you?"

"Maybe a few rich boys like you," Derrick answered, his voice thick with contempt.

"Wait a minute. I've never been to Maui. That's a pretty expensive place for you to be taking me."

"They're taking you, I'm not," he spat out. A second later, realizing what he had admitted, Derrick's body tensed. He took three strides across the room and shoved Michael hard against the dresser. "You're done packing," he snarled.

"All right," Michael said, holding both hands up in the air, fearing the man as much as the .38. He grabbed his bag as Derrick pushed him toward the hall.

Once in the living room, Derrick commanded Michael to sit down. Jaws twitching, the bodyguard stood looking out the living room window, waiting with watchdog obedience. Lee was inside the car, apparently on the phone.

Michael wiped a weak hand across his clammy forehead. In a few minutes he would be a bona fide prisoner and no one would know. He certainly couldn't sneak in a phone call, and he'd already ruled out making a run for it. Only a long shot was left. He picked up a pencil and piece of paper from the coffee table.

"Put that down," Derrick growled.

"I need to leave a note. Someone needs to take care of my cat."

A sardonic smile came to Derrick's face, as if this time he had it over Michael. "Write what you want. I'll have Lee read it."

Dependent on Lee. He couldn't think for himself. Michael wondered if Derrick had Lee pick out his socks, too.

Five minutes later the door swung open. "Ready?" Lee asked impatiently.

"He wrote something," Derrick said, motioning toward the coffee table. "You better read it." Lee glanced at Michael and then walked over and picked up the note.

A moment later Lee threw the paper back on the table, obviously annoyed. "It's two sentences about his pet. Why couldn't you have read it? Or can't you read?" he asked sarcastically.

While Lee reproved Derrick with a debasing glare, Michael pulled something out of his pocket and slid it behind a picture frame. For a moment he thought Lee had noticed, and fear bottled up tight in his throat. But the fair-skinned man only strode out the door, demanding that they follow. They did . . . Derrick with a scowl on his face and Michael praying fervently that Marissa would remember.

Five

Marissa arrived at work a few minutes early, hoping to make amends with Trish, the impatient young hostess. She headed directly for the break room, stowed her sweater in a locker deemed hers by a piece of tape with M.T. written in blue ink, and walked quickly down the hall toward the podium. She didn't get far.

"Tomsen?" John barked from his office. Marissa turned back reluctantly. "Sorry to interrupt your mad dash, but we need to talk." The sarcasm in John's voice was predictable. Everyone tolerated him, but nobody liked him. His obnoxious, rude, and egocentric character was crammed all in one short, stocky package. An ugly, yellowing shark's tooth necklace hung around his neck, and he reeked of cheap cologne and cigarette smoke. He claimed to be married, although even in the short time Marissa had worked with him, two women had asked directions to his office, each saying she was his girlfriend. Marissa wondered what they saw in him.

John's office was in its usual cluttered state, and when he motioned her in, she had to move an overflowing ash tray off the only other chair to sit down.

"How's work?" he asked, making no effort to hide his physical interest for her.

"Fine."

"I can't decide whether I want to go out with you or have

you as an employee. Or maybe we could do both."

"Is this what you wanted to talk to me about?"

John chuckled. "Not in the mood, huh?" Then he paused and his voice turned serious. "Does the name Spencer Mitchell mean anything to you?"

Marissa's eyes roamed the office before reluctantly returning to his. "He works for the hotel, right?"

"You could say that. He's the hotel manager. My boss." John let Spencer's title sink in before he went on. "He asked me to have you fill out a police report," he said, handing her a multiple carbon form. "Should this concern me?"

"No," Marissa said.

"No? Is that all you're going to say?"

Marissa didn't need any suspicions cast on her, so she thought it best to play it safe and tell him what he wanted to hear. "I was mugged on one of the Regency's elevators."

"By the jewel thief? The guy who's been hitting the nice hotels?" John appeared excited, as if an article in one of his many copies of *Enquirer* had come to life. "How did he do it? Did he point his gun right at you?"

"He pretty much stayed out of sight."

"So you didn't see anything?"

"Just a bag lowered down for our valuables."

Marissa's calm explanation seemed to bring John's concerns back to present. "That robbery happened on Tuesday," he said, looking over at a schedule thumbtacked to the wall. "You were scheduled to work. Who filled in for you?"

"No one," Marissa said evenly.

John looked at her as though she was trying to pull one over on him, which in Marissa's mind wouldn't have been difficult, but he seemed upset by the notion. "The robbery happened just before my shift," Marissa said. "I clocked in less than fifteen minutes late."

John rolled his eyes at her response. "Right. You couldn't have worked after something like that."

"No one was hurt. It really wasn't a big deal."

"Did you grow up in inner-city L.A. or something?"

Marissa glanced at her watch. "I need to relieve Trish. Her boyfriend's probably waiting for her. Are we finished?"

"No, there's one more thing," John said, the robbery seeming to ease out of his mind as his eyes ran up and down her body. "The hotel gives each department manager two tickets to the King Kamehameha party. It's ritzy . . . something you'd enjoy." He gave her a slow smile. "You could go with me."

"No, thank you," she said, standing.

John didn't appear affected by her refusal and only shuffled through some papers, then ran his finger across one. "Let's see, you're near the bottom of the pay scale. Going with me could probably get you a little increase." He paused and looked up, giving her the opportunity to reconsider. "Well, the party isn't for two weeks," he quickly added as she turned for the door. "Think about it, okay?"

Marissa walked to the podium shaking her head and imagining what some of her girlfriends back home would say. After spewing sexual harassment charges to volcanic proportions, they'd be angry that she wasn't reporting him. But right now she had more important things on her mind. Besides, she knew legal action would do John little good. What he needed was a new heart.

ȵ ȵ ȵ ȵ

After four hours of seating a steady flow of customers, Marissa welcomed her dinner break. She headed straight to the women's lounge and sank down on one of the overstuffed chairs next to the floor-to-ceiling, wall-to-wall mirror. She still wasn't used to being on her feet for hours at a time, and her shoes felt like they were a half size too small.

Lynn Roth, a solidly built synthetic blonde appeared from the washroom area. "I see you've found our only hiding place from Mr. Worthless," she said, sitting down on a padded bench opposite Marissa. She pulled a pack of cigarettes from her uniform's side pocket and tapped the box several times before one slid out. "Of course, one of these days I just know he's going to come flying through that door no matter what the sign says."

"Talking about John?" Marissa asked, a smirk raising the corners of her mouth.

"The one and hopefully only. If there is another man like him, give me a handgun." Lynn was coarse and straightforward—a combination of traits that made her likable in Marissa's eyes. She'd befriended Marissa immediately, offering bits of advice and answering questions she'd been asked repeatedly in the nine years she'd waitressed. She lit the cigarette, took a long drag, and turned toward the mirror, looking at herself critically.

"What I need is a haircut," Lynn said, blowing a stream of smoke out the corner of her mouth. "Finding the time and money is another thing. I've got three kids and a lazy ex who won't pay child support." She pulled a few bobby pins from her pocket and began fussing with her hair. "Do you have any kids?"

Marissa shook her head.

"A boyfriend?"

"We broke up a few weeks ago. It was for the best."

"A loser, huh?"

"Something like that," Marissa said. Donald had been far from a loser. He was bright, handsome, on his way up the corporate ladder, and a gentleman, as well. She thought he had been the real thing. The memories of their relationship were still fresh and painful, and Marissa saw no advantage sharing the details with someone she'd only known three days.

"Put your feet up," Lynn commented, nodding toward a nearby stool. "They'll feel better."

"Is my pain that obvious?" Marissa questioned, directing a smile to her new friend.

"Everyone gets sore feet the first few days," Lynn said. She took another puff of her cigarette. "What they need is some time in the whirlpool. We're not supposed to use the facilities, but you can always use the 'I'm new and didn't know' excuse."

Marissa wondered if she should. Her throbbing feet told her yes. "Where is it?"

"Mezzanine floor. South side."

"Maybe I'll just dip them in for a few minutes," Marissa said, standing and then absentmindedly waving at the smoke near her face.

"My smoking bothers you, huh?"

"I like fresh air better," Marissa admitted.

"I should quit," Lynn said with a sigh. "I certainly don't need the expense."

"Well, then, enjoy your last one," Marissa quipped, smiling as she walked toward the door.

"You think it's that easy?" Lynn complained.

"I never said that."

"Hey, don't be late," Lynn warned. "John's here tonight."

Marissa nodded as she walked out the door and down the hall. She didn't know whether to laugh or cry. Scheduled breaks, timecards, a boss who hired on looks—her life had changed overnight. Only last month she'd been handling half-a-million-dollar advertising campaigns. She wasn't management level, but she was advancing well. Hard work, a flair for distinctive copy, and being honest with clients had helped her excel, and she'd merited a huge office overlooking the Willamette River. By the world's standards she appeared successful, but there was something missing from her life that she yearned for. It wasn't the desire to get married and have children, although some day she wanted to. It was something else. Something she couldn't put her finger on.

Relieved no one else was using the outdoor Jacuzzi, Marissa sat on the cement edge and slipped her tired feet in the swirling, therapeutic water. As a couple approached she thought to remove her name tag so her employee status wouldn't be so evident. The two weren't ones to notice, though. They were obviously mesmerized with each other, laughing softly, walking arm-in-arm, looking at no one but each other. Was that the way she had been with Donald? At least in the beginning?

She couldn't help but smile as she thought back. There was something magnetic about Donald. They had met at a company Christmas party, between the champagne fountain and the sushi bar. Afterward he'd convinced her to go out to a midnight breakfast with him and then for a stroll through the Rose Garden. She didn't want the evening to end. A week later, he catered a four-course dinner in her office complete with a concert violinist. And once, after a rare snowstorm, he'd made a snowman in her yard holding a dozen red roses. She had fallen hard for him.

Then came the talk that her advancement in the company was because of her dating Donald. Her close friends knew better. If anything, her relationship with Donald, the newly chosen vice president of Jonah Stevens, was more of a detriment—especially with her brother.

Michael didn't see the qualities in Donald she did, and on the rare occasions when Michael's and Donald's paths crossed, the tension was as thick as an Oregonian redwood. Marissa had no idea why the ill will, other than personality differences—Donald being a perfectionist and Michael the more spontaneous type.

But it was Donald's casual indifference to Christianity that brought her back down from the clouds. Donald attended church, but Marissa knew that being a member of a large congregation and attending a few church council meetings simply rounded out his public image. When she asked him about his faith, he told her his spirituality was more internal and that it was difficult to put into words. Not until a few weeks ago had she allowed herself to honestly see the reality of dating someone who didn't share her deepest conviction.

Thankfully, Donald was in Chicago when she requested her three weeks of vacation plus additional time without pay if she so needed. By claiming her need "personal," she avoided many questions, and because of her good organizational skills the process of transferring her work to others went smoothly. Too smoothly. Heartsick, she handed over the much anticipated

Pepsi promotional project—what would have been her biggest campaign yet. She didn't call Donald until she was at the airport.

"You're leaving, just like that?" Donald said. He sounded offended. "What about the Pepsi promo?! It's big for the company. It's big for you. I can't believe you'd do this to the firm . . . and what about us?"

Yes, and what about them? He'd voiced his concern for the company first, making his priorities all too glaring. Still, she knew it was a shock for him and a definite wrong career move for her. But she didn't have a choice.

"I know. I'm sorry, but I wouldn't leave if this wasn't important."

"What is it? What's so important?"

"I can't go into it. I'm sorry."

"Can't go into it? I'm your boyfriend. What kind of an answer is that?"

"It's the only one I have," Marissa said, suddenly feeling tired—both physically and mentally. The last few days had been nearly overwhelming. "Anyway," she said, forcing the words, "some time away from each other will probably be best."

"Best?" he said disconcertingly. "Best for whom?"

"For both of us," Marissa said, her heart twisting as her eyes took in a nearby couple's embrace. She was glad Donald was a thousand miles away. Only last month she had been about to end the relationship, but he'd finessed his way around some issues and she'd taken him back.

"Tell me what's wrong," Donald offered. "If it's us, I think we're just going through a slump. All couples do some time or the other. Move in with me. It'll be better. I promise."

Marissa blinked back tears. How many times had Donald suggested they live together, as if cohabiting would cure everything? "You know I'd never do that. I have morals, unlike Rebecca."

"Why do you keep throwing her in my face? I've apologized for that night over and over. What more can I do?"

There was nothing he could do. He had broken her trust. Nothing could bring that back.

"Boarding will begin now for flight twenty-eight," the intercom announced. "Please have your boarding passes ready. Seating will—"

"Marissa, don't go," Donald blurted. "I love you."

For the first time nothing happened to her heart when he said those words. His unfaithfulness had been terribly hard on her. She'd discovered what he was . . . or rather, what he wasn't. Empty and so very sad, she felt a lone tear run down her cheek.

"I'm sorry, Donald." Her voice was barely audible now. She would miss his voice, his touch, his kiss. Her soul ached with the first pangs of loneliness.

"I'm coming home in just a few hours," Donald said, taking control. "Stay there. Don't get on that plane. We have to talk." Marissa shook her head no, and with a numb heart, she hung up the phone and walked onto the waiting plane.

Six

*A*fter two hours of asking about Michael's pendant in La-haina's many jewelry shops, Marissa finally found a jeweler who nodded in recognition.

"Looks like Gabe's work to me," he said, studying the piece through his loupe. "He used to do repairs for us, but he was best known for his etchings. Gabriel Hawkins was his name."

"Was?"

"Yeah. Too bad about him. He died last year in a house fire." The jeweler handed the necklace back to her.

"Did he make any others like it?"

"Doubt it," he replied, shaking his head. "He only sold originals. Had customers who'd wait months to buy his stuff. He could have made a fortune if he'd mass-produced. But he always refused." The jeweler shrugged. "Must have had his reasons, I guess." The bell on the front door sounded and he looked away. "I have to take care of a delivery. Look around. We have lots of other etchings."

Disappointed in discovering another dead end, Marissa returned to the condo, tossed her straw purse on the couch, and walked out onto the lanai overlooking the hot tub and two pools, which sat in the middle of the horseshoe-shaped complex. It was mid-afternoon and the sky was a radiant blue. A dozen or so people, mainly couples, lounged around the area. Their relaxed state looked inviting.

Feelings of guilt that she wasn't doing enough to find Michael had prohibited her from enjoying much of anything—including sunbathing. But today she felt different. Today she was angry at her brother and frustrated over her situation—especially since she had no idea if she was pursuing the right path. What more could she do than a private investigator could?

Every time she saw a Pepsi can in someone's hand, she grieved over her decision about taking time off from Jonah Stevens. When she returned to work, it would no doubt take double the months of hard work and devotion to earn another chance with a major client.

Of course, Michael was more important to her than a job, but she couldn't help remembering the lottery tickets she would see every once in a while in his pocket. And then there was that trip to Las Vegas he had taken just a few months earlier. He said he wasn't going there to gamble, but when he came back he spoke little of what he had done. If she had given up the much coveted Pepsi promo because Michael had gambled their money away and now had run away because he was too ashamed to show his face . . . She jammed a few things into her beach bag, slipped on her swimsuit, and walked out of the condo. For her own sanity, she needed some time for herself.

Marissa walked down the wide, outdoor staircase that led to a path across the immaculate grounds, and only after she reached the fence surrounding the pool did she remember that each guest was required to use a key. She sighed deeply and moved closer to the hibiscus hedge, searching her bag for the elusive key ring. "Oww," she said when a prickly branch from the hedge scratched her arm.

"Forgot your key?" a man's voice asked. Startled, Marissa looked up to see Spencer Mitchell dressed in swim trunks and sandals, a towel across one shoulder. Something about the curve of his mouth and his compelling blue eyes made her stare a second longer than she wanted to.

"No, it's in here somewhere," Marissa said, looking back into her tote, continuing the search. Of all the people on the island, why did she have to run into Spencer? No doubt he was going to ask her about the police report she had no intentions of completing.

"This might be quicker," Spencer said, unlocking the iron-rod gate with his own key, then stepping aside to let her walk in first.

"Thanks," Marissa said, nodding only briefly before she chose a chair close to the fence and next to another chair that had a book and pair of sunglasses on it. Since the chair obviously belonged to someone, she expected him to walk by. Instead, he stopped, picked up the book, slipped on the glasses, and sat down. Marissa cringed inwardly. When would this day end?

"So you live here?" Spencer asked, appearing unaware of her disgruntled feelings toward him.

"I moved in a couple weeks ago," Marissa said, avoiding eye contact as she attempted to adjust her chair.

"I haven't been here long, either. Used to have a place in Kihei, but I hated fighting the traffic to work. No need to sell you, though. You're probably here for the same reason."

"Yeah," she agreed, pulling harder on the back of the chair, trying to bring it forward.

"Here," he said, leaning over to help. "These chairs can be stubborn." In one fluid motion, he pushed the chair all the way down and then back up to a reclining position.

"Thank you," she murmured, allowing her eyes a quick glance his way. After slipping off her sandals, she busied herself with spreading her beach towel over her chair.

"It's pretty expensive to live here," Spencer commented, watching her. "You must have a roommate, huh?"

Marissa leaned back against the blanketed chair as a warning sounded in her head. Why would he ask such a question? He already had a girlfriend, so he most likely wouldn't be after a date. Could he somehow be involved in Michael's disappearance?

"That's a little personal, isn't it?" she finally said.

"Guess you're right," Spencer noted with a shrug. "I just

thought it might be tight trying to live here on a hostess's salary."

"Maybe you think too much," Marissa said, hoping to end his desire for conversation. It did. She could see the kindness drain from his eyes, and she felt horrible when he picked up his book, no doubt having understood her attitude and its message. She felt like apologizing. Spencer most likely knew her hourly wage and was simply curious as to how she could afford to live here. Still, common sense held the words back. Her situation wasn't wise to share, no matter how innocent the question. She put a dab of sunscreen on her nose, slipped on a visor, and closed her eyes.

Despite the tropical conditions, Marissa couldn't relax. Spencer's comment reminded her of her financial situation, and she began adding up bills in her mind, wondering again if she should have rented out her parents' house. Neither she nor Michael had had the heart to allow strangers to live there. At least not until they made a final decision whether to sell it.

The well-maintained family home looked like a smaller version of Tara in *Gone With the Wind*. Their parents' dream had been to take in foster kids and expose them to a place where they didn't have to worry about their troubled lives, a place where they could run free in the woods surrounding the house and simply be kids. They had only just begun taking in children when the accident happened. Their unattained dream had been one more reason Marissa had a hard time accepting their death. What good had come from God's taking them so soon?

Spencer's chair grated on the concrete and she opened her eyes. "Excuse me," he mumbled as he brushed her leg. A moment later he dived into the pool. Marissa watched in fascination as he swam lap after lap. She admired his perfect form and wondered how he could swim so effortlessly when she had such a fear of the water. She couldn't even float.

Five years ago she'd signed up for a swimming class at the YMCA, thinking it was time she learned. But as she stood by the heavily chlorinated pool, shivering in her damp swimsuit, fear convinced her otherwise and she slipped back to the locker room, changed, and never went back. Since then, she'd avoided water deeper than her shoulders. It didn't matter that much anyway, she surmised. Her last two vacations hadn't included much pool time.

After several laps, Spencer pulled himself out of the water. He acknowledged her as he toweled off and returned to his chair, but then he looked back to the pool, contemplative. "I don't know about you," he began, "but I've thought a lot about the robbery—what could have happened. Guess I feel fortunate no one was hurt." He paused and looked over at her. "Did you read about the Sheraton incident?"

Marissa had. The crime had been played out the same way, only someone tried to act heroic and two people had been shot. One died at the hospital, the other was in critical condition. The death was sudden, just as her parents' deaths had been, and she couldn't help but consider the remaining family. She'd even prayed for them. But Marissa couldn't share this. She felt that in order to protect herself—especially in her fragile emotional state—she had to keep her distance. "In yesterday's paper?" she found herself saying. "Yeah. I read it."

"Yeah, you read it?" Spencer asked, his face a study of disbelief. "Didn't you drop to your knees that night and thank God it wasn't you?"

Marissa readjusted her visor. "I think you're getting personal again."

Her comment seemed to push him into an authoritarian role. "Whether or not you give a rip about nearly getting killed is your business. My business is getting everyone who was on that elevator to fill out a report. John gave you the paper work, didn't he?"

"Yes," Marissa said, "but I don't need my jewelry back, and you four witnessed the same thing I did so there's no reason for me to get involved."

"There is a reason." Spencer's voice heightened in intensity as he continued. "I told the police there were five people on the elevator, and they expect five reports."

"Tell them you miscounted."

"Should I give the police your name and address?"

Marissa paused a moment before replying calmly. "If that's what you feel you have to do."

"What is it with you? Are you bitter at everyone, or just me?"

So she appeared bitter . . . a small price to pay if it would allow her privacy. "I think I've had enough sun," Marissa concluded, slipping on her sandals and gathering her belongings. As she picked up her tote and stood, something reflected brightly on the concrete near her feet and she looked down. Somehow Michael's pendant had slipped out. Admonishing herself for being so careless, she bent to retrieve it, but Spencer's hand closed over it first.

"This is yours?" he said, leaning back, looking at the piece with interest and examining the insignia closer.

Was that recognition on his face? Marissa's internal alarm sounded again, this time louder.

"May I have it, please?" she asked nervously, needing to regain the small link to her brother.

Spencer studied the pendant a moment longer, slowly fingering its unique design, then handed it back.

"Thank you," she said, hesitating a moment as his direct gaze caught her eye. Then she quickly turned and walked away. Breathing a sigh of relief once the hedgerow hid her from view, she started back down the path toward her condo, but then she paused and turned the other direction.

Pushing open the door to the condominium office, Marissa walked up to the counter and caught the attention of a heavy-set woman behind the desk. Marissa felt awkward about asking, but her nagging suspicion forced her to speak.

"My name is Marissa Tomsen, and I'm in 208. I just met a man named Spencer Mitchell and I was . . . well, I was wondering how long he's lived here. At least he says he lives here."

"I think I remember that name," the woman said, moving

her glasses up on her nose as she looked through the Rolodex. "Let's see . . . M . . . Mitchell. Yes, he's in 108. Looks like he moved in on the twelfth. You don't have a complaint, do you?"

"No, I—" Marissa hesitated. "Actually, I thought he was nice looking."

"Oh, I see," the older woman chuckled. "Well, good luck."

Marissa smiled back, but her gaiety disappeared the moment she turned for the door. Spencer Mitchell moved in four days after she had and occupied the condo directly under hers. The situation seemed more than coincidental.

Seven

Michael opened his eyes as he lay on the lumpy mattress of the motel room. It was almost midnight. Derrick, his ever-faithful bodyguard, had his twin bed butted up to the door. He'd handcuffed one of Michael's feet to the bed and removed the phone. *Oh yes,* he thought sarcastically, *this is a great way to promote human potential.*

By now, the reality of the manipulative messages he'd been fed were staring him in the face. He'd had time enough to think about his financial commitment, the controlled environment of the classes, the trip to Las Vegas. . . . What a scam! What had he been thinking?

The problem was, he hadn't been thinking. He'd been so consumed with the promises—especially about investing to obtain financial security and being able to retire at forty. And there had been the job offer as a media consultant with Ekvar—a supposedly up-and-coming investment company. The pay and perks were outstanding, with none of the stress of deadlines like at the *Tribune.*

Then out of the blue a letter arrived. No return address. It simply said: *Scam company. Don't take the offer.*

Michael made a few phone calls, one even to the FBI, inquiring about Ekvar. They made no accusations, but they did say some members of the company had been indicted. This information and the letter made Michael decline the offer. Shortly after that, he'd been abducted.

If only he had known that Ekvar, the Bible class, and the self-improvement class were all linked. He could see now how Lee and his deceiving group infiltrated their scam through New Covenant Church. The church was so large and had so many evening Bible classes that the pastor or council didn't have the time to attend each one. Or, even if they did, they were most likely unaware that the so-called Bible study's second semester was a self-improvement course that encouraged participants to invest with Ekvar.

These scam artists knew exactly what they were doing, and the church was tragically unaware. Some way or another he was going to get out of here, get his money back, and blow the operation wide open. Maybe the story would even get front page coverage. They couldn't keep him forever. Sooner or later, they'd have to release him.

He'd scratched his name in code on numerous walls and bathroom stalls—everywhere they had been so later he could prove where they had confined him. He'd nearly escaped when they moved the classes to an out-of-the-way building in an industrial area, but he'd ended up trapped in a locked stairwell.

Suddenly someone knocked loudly on the motel door next to his and then entered. At first he was bothered by the voices. He wanted to sleep. Then he thought he heard someone say his name. Slowly, Michael sat up. He kept an eye on the sleeping muscleman as he cautiously slid to the end of the bed toward the locked door that separated the rooms, anguishing over every squeak the bed made. Stretching as far as his confinement would allow, he was able to put his ear near the space in the molding. He strained to hear what was being said.

"So what happened?" a voice said. Michael immediately recognized it as Lee's.

"I don't know," a deeper voice answered, then swore profusely. "We wined and dined him in Las Vegas, told him about the resorts. He sounded like he'd do it. Has no family, either.

Parents died. Has a sister, but he said they don't get along. Out of the blue he says he wants to bail." More swearing. "Steve said too bad he'd already told the big boys he was our new guy. So he will be. You know Steve. When he found out about the estate, the money, and his reporter skills, he wanted him. Only thing was, he didn't take the position. Steve still insisted we'd found ourselves a golden goose."

"I don't know how golden he is," Lee observed. "He's not cooperating."

"You brought him over here by force. What did you expect?"

Lee swore. "I was told to. Anyway, now it's too late."

"And now we're stuck with the problem," the deeper voice added.

"We can remediate him. I'll call Star."

"She's a worthless crack head."

"Her hypnosis works," Lee remarked.

"Do whatever it takes. A lot is riding on this." Michael heard footsteps toward the outer door. Then they paused, and the deeper-voiced man spoke again. "You know that if the site isn't set up in two months, Steve will have the boys feed our bodies to the sharks in Kineioli Bay. You better not mess up." The door quickly opened and then shut. All was quiet except for Michael's heart pounding double time in his chest. He moved away from the door to get circulation back into his confined foot.

What does all this mean? Michael's brain worked to piece everything together. They made a mistake but now it was too late? What did they mean by too late? Feeling feverish, he didn't know if it was because of the flu or this ill-fated news.

Hypnosis? The thought of someone messing with his thoughts terrified him. Never! Never would he allow anyone to hypnotize him. Then the horrible thought came to him that maybe this Star person could do it without his cooperation. Maybe drugs or some strange herbs were used to induce a relaxed state.

Michael heard Lee talking again. He strained to put his ear to the door.

"I need to talk to Star," Lee was saying. There was a pause. "I don't care what she's doing! Have her meet me at the motel now!" Then the phone slammed down with a crash.

The hypnotist was coming! Adrenaline flowing, Michael moved back on the bed, no longer caring about squeaks or movements that may waken Derrick. Was there something he could do short of trying to pull the attached bed to Derrick's, knock him out, get the keys, and run? He knew even the first action was impossible since the headboard was bolted to the wall.

He looked toward the nightstand near his bed. They no doubt had emptied it, but he opened it anyway. A Bible. He stared at it, a sense of peace descending upon his senses. Just knowing something good and pure was in the room with him brought some comfort. Holding the Bible—its solid weight resting comfortably in his hand—felt right, and it reminded him again about the handouts in the Bible class. For all he knew now, maybe the words they had "copied" weren't from the Bible at all. He didn't know the verses well enough to judge.

He began reading the Psalms, the serenity as quenching as a much-needed drink of water. "The Lord is my rock, my fortress and my deliverer. . . ." The words sounded strong and sure—exactly opposite of how he felt. He continued reading, but too soon he heard approaching footsteps. Quickly, he pulled open the drawer and began to return the book, but then he hesitated. He didn't want to let it go. Impulsively, he slid the Bible underneath him. He knew the book itself had no power, but he knew it contained God's Word. He wanted to be reminded—maybe even uncomfortably—that God was more powerful than these people.

The pounding on the door a few seconds later produced a moan from Derrick. More pounding motivated Derrick to stand and move the bed away from the entry door. Michael tried to prepare himself. He acted sleepy.

Lee strode into the room with a woman who was dressed like a twenty-year-old but looked more like she was pushing fifty. Her short black skirt looked as cheap as her makeup job. There was no explanation of why she was there. Michael let out a sigh, closed his eyes, and pretended to fall back asleep. He hoped she wouldn't use drugs.

With his shoulders resting on the Bible underneath, Michael prayed as the woman began her incantation.

Eight

After Marissa stowed her blazer in the break room, she heard John talking to one of the new waitresses in his office. Marissa paused out of view but within hearing range, pretending to adjust her name tag.

"So do you want to go with me?" Marissa heard John asking.

"To a company party?" The young waitress's voice sounded unsure. "It won't be like . . . anything weird, right?"

"It's high class. You'll probably see more diamonds there than you have in your entire life."

"I don't know."

John lowered his voice. "You could probably get a little increase in your hourly pay."

"A raise, just for going?" There was a brief silence. "Oh, all right," she finally said.

Marissa shook her head. John must have figured that she wouldn't go to the party and decided to ask the long-legged lovely he'd just hired. *At least I don't have to worry about him bringing up the party again*, Marissa thought as she hurried to the podium.

Turning the corner, she collided with a solidly built body. She stiffened automatically when she realized who it was.

"My fault," Spencer said, his voice quietly husky.

"No, it was mine," she said, knowing it had been. His eyes,

gazing down upon her, were kind and decent. Caught unaware, Marissa allowed a gentle smile to grace her features. But then she remembered. She had to be careful around him. She dropped her eyes and moved to walk past.

"Wait," he said, halting her steps. "I was looking for you. We need to talk."

"I can't. My shift is just beginning." Marissa didn't need another interrogation, personal or otherwise.

"It won't take long."

"Spencer!" John called, walking out of his office. "Do you need something from me?" An uncharacteristic sincerity rang from his voice.

"Actually, I'd like to talk with Marissa. It should only take a few minutes."

"No problem," John said, his obsequious self slithering through. "Sit anywhere. I'll send Lynn over with some coffee."

Marissa walked across the dining room and chose a table with the best view, knowing that in just a few minutes there would be patrons eager to sit there. If Spencer had any business sense, he would cut the conversation short.

Lynn was quick to bring the coffee. She gave Marissa an I'm-dying-to-know-what-this-is-about look as she walked away.

"Perfect day for sailing," Spencer said, gazing out the window toward the water. "But then, everyday is perfect in paradise, isn't it?" His comment did nothing to temper the strained atmosphere between them, neither did it invoke a conversation. He took a sip of coffee and looked over at her. "You mentioned earlier that you were new to the island. What brought you to Maui?"

This wasn't fair, his being able to interrogate her under the guise of employer. His questions would eventually lead to Michael.

"Do you normally interview people after they've accepted the job?" Marissa inquired.

"I wouldn't call this an interview."

"Then what would you call it?"

Spencer leaned back in his chair. "I need some answers from you."

"Why I came to Maui is my own business."

"Maybe." Goose bumps appeared on her arms. Could he know about Michael? But before she could entertain the idea, his voice continued. "At the pool I noticed you had the same necklace as the one you supposedly gave up during the robbery."

"You're quite the observer," she said evenly.

"Maybe you can explain how you managed to get it back."

"I don't know why I have to explain anything," Marissa commented, increasing her resolve for privacy.

"Let's see," Spencer said, holding up his hand to tick off points. "You refused to fill out a police report. John says you returned to work after the mugging acting as if nothing out of the ordinary happened. You admit you lost nothing important. Then, I see a necklace fall out of your purse that looks like the one you had to give up on the elevator." He paused. "All those facts lead me to believe you were an insider."

"In on the robbery?" She hadn't expected this.

He shrugged, his shoulders waiting for her defense.

"I may not be telling you my life story, but I'm not a criminal." Her expression changed from defiance to exasperation. "You're right, I refused the police report and I wasn't that shaken up, but that's not a crime. Neither is not losing anything important. As for the necklace, I wanted to keep it so I let it slip down my blouse."

"You what?" Spencer asked incredulously. "The guy had a gun. If he had noticed he might have shot you or any of us."

"Well, he didn't." Marissa couldn't meet his eyes.

"I find it disturbing that you'd risk your life and everyone else's over a cheap necklace."

Marissa swallowed hard. "I thought the guy was bluffing. I had no idea he actually had a gun." She paused. "I understand your position, though, so I'll work here just until John can find a replacement. Or I could quit immediately. Whatever you want."

Spencer gave her a long, hard look and then turned his gaze toward the ocean and sighed.

For a moment Marissa considered how Spencer's theory about her had validity, even if it wasn't true. She thought how ironic it was that the tables had turned from her thinking he was the enemy to him thinking the same about her. It was then she noticed how tired he looked . . . like he'd been up all night. He was most likely under tremendous pressure being the manager of a hotel that had just been robbed. Yesterday she heard a couple say that they were checking out of their room two days early because they were afraid to ride the elevators. She wondered if he was worried about other things as well. When Spencer finally turned back, she lowered her eyes. Her job was most likely history.

"If you're willing to give us enough information for a security background check, I'll let you stay," Spencer finally said.

"What would that entail?" Marissa said, relieved that she might be able to keep her job and yet still reluctant to provide personal information.

"For starters," Spencer said, pulling a pen from his chest pocket, "I'd like the name of your former employer."

Marissa studied his face for a moment, hoping she was doing the right thing. Her financial situation forced the compromise. "Jonah Stevens Advertising Agency," she said. "Portland, Oregon." He wrote the name and the telephone number she gave him on a cocktail napkin.

"All right, then," Spencer concluded, pushing back his chair and standing. "If you pass, you can stay."

"Wait," Marissa suddenly said as he turned to leave.

He turned back and looked at her expectantly.

"I have a request," Marissa said, her voice weak. "When you call Jonah Stevens, could you please not mention where I am and what position I have? I . . . I'd rather they didn't know."

Spencer held her eyes for a moment and then, not committing himself to anything, simply walked away.

🐝　🐝　🐝　🐝

"No. Spencer does not like me," Marissa told Lynn on their break. "The truth is, he doesn't trust me. He thinks I'm part of the elevator robbery ring."

"You've got to be kidding."

Marissa shook her head. "He's going to check up on me call the last place I worked."

"Will they vouch for you?"

"As long as he doesn't talk with my ex-boyfriend. He works there."

"Might give him an earful, huh?" Lynn said with a chuckle. "Well, you'll have to live with Spencer knowing all about you because it'll be impossible to avoid him. He eats here every Saturday night, rain or shine."

Marissa rolled her eyes. "Great."

Lynn reached for another cigarette, but then pushed it back into the pack. "You're right about smoking. I should quit. And *I'm* right about you needing a night out. A group of us are going to The Crescent Moon tonight. Why don't you come along? It's a private club. Great dancing. Plenty of men. One of my friends knows the owner."

"I don't know," Marissa said, hesitant.

Lynn picked up her cigarettes again and began pulling one out. "Okay, okay," Marissa relented, holding up her hands. "Put them away. I'll go. This is all for the sake of your health, you know."

🐝　🐝　🐝　🐝

Fluorescent neon shaped into hula dancers and geckos lit up the club's crowded dance floor. Marissa sat at a corner table nursing a Pepsi, straining to hear Lynn and her friends over the blaring band. The group seemed nice enough, but they frequently digressed into pidgin English and tasteless jokes. Marissa attempted a laugh now and then, but her heart wasn't in it. She began to wonder why she'd agreed to come at all—bar atmospheres always seemed base to her. She couldn't help but wish she were with her friends in Portland. Drinking coffee on a rainy afternoon at Tom's Bakery was more enjoyable than this.

Marissa felt a tap on her arm and looked across the table toward a man with slicked-back hair and full lips, toying idly with his glass. "Want to dance?" he said.

"No thanks," she said, not liking the self-satisfaction in his eyes. "I've danced with tourists all day."

"I'm better than a tourist," he said with a leer.

"Leave her alone, Phil," Lynn said. "She just broke up with her boyfriend. She's not interested."

When the second round of drinks arrived, so did another one of Lynn's friends. "Marissa, this is Rita," Lynn said, pulling a chair over for the slender blonde. "Marissa is a new hostess," Lynn explained. "She's a writer, too."

"Really?" Rita said, obviously interested. "What do you write?"

Marissa smiled self-consciously. When Lynn began asking too many questions about what brought her to Maui, Marissa told her she needed time to research and write. Lynn jumped to the conclusion that she was writing a book and Marissa didn't correct her. The "book" provided plenty of excuses about what she did in her spare time, why friends arranged for her stay in the condo, and why she could afford to work only part time. Tonight was her first snag.

"I'm working on a piece of fiction," Marissa said, playing the part despite her discomfort, "but it probably won't go anywhere. What do you write?"

"Poetry, but it probably won't go anywhere, either." They both laughed.

"I think you're both going to be famous," Lynn said, raising her glass. "And when the money starts rolling in, I know you'll remember me."

"You're always thinking about money," Rita teased.

"Look who's talking," Lynn said. "You're a travel agent. You make great money *and* get to go places. I have to depend on generous patrons."

"All you have to do is enroll in the travel college I told you about," Rita said. "They have classes to fit your schedule, and it really isn't that much money. You could do it. I know you could."

"Sounds like a good idea," Marissa said, looking expectantly at Lynn.

"What are you guys," Lynn said with a frown, "my career planners? This is my night out—I plan on enjoying it." Lynn glared at Rita as though the two had battled this topic before, and the subject was dropped.

"I'm going out for some fresh air," Marissa said an hour later, motioning to the lanai. Lynn nodded and Marissa weaved her way through the tables and out past the wide-open double doors, relieved to exchange the smoke-filled air for the ocean's refreshing breeze. Standing next to a row of large potted plants that separated one club's lanai from the other, she stared at the couples who walked hand in hand along the mile-long strip of beach. Maui's paradise wasn't in the bar. It was out here.

As the light breeze caressed her face, she tried to find pleasure over not needing the thick sweater, slicker, and boots she'd be wearing if she were home. But the thoughts didn't satisfy her as they usually did on winter vacations. Perfect weather and tropical surroundings couldn't take away her worries about Michael or satisfy her longing for the fellowship of close friends or—for Donald. Despite his unfaithfulness, a part of her still loved him. A few times she'd been tempted to call him. Once she even dialed his number but then quickly hung up.

By now Donald had seen her letter requesting leave without pay. He would no doubt be angry over her absence, especially since he had no way to get a hold of her. *This is best*, she kept reminding herself. She must try to hold fast to her decision about ending their relationship. She knew she had done the right thing and trusted there was someone else for her, someone who held high her same beliefs. She would wait.

It was then that voices from the other side of the dense bushes caught her attention and she found herself straining to hear.

"I need more time," a man was saying.

"You've had enough time," a woman reprimanded. "We'll handle this now."

"No," the man insisted. "This is my client. I'll follow through."

Marissa's eyes darted to her left, but she couldn't see through the thick foliage. Was it only her imagination, or did the man's voice sound familiar?

"You have one more week," the woman hissed. "Find her or you're dead."

Marissa gripped the railing as heavy footsteps thudded down the outer staircase. Standing as though a statue, she waited for lighter steps to follow. When they didn't, an odd sensation tingled through her, as though some alien entity was hovering nearby. Finally, she looked back to her left. Some of the bushes had been forced apart, revealing a pair of hateful, venomous eyes staring at her.

"Eavesdropping?" the red-lipped mouth whispered.

Marissa gasped and ran back into the club, the sinister tone of the woman's voice echoing in her ears.

Nine

Marissa felt a knot in her stomach when Spencer walked in the restaurant Saturday evening. Ever since John told her she had passed the security check, she'd wondered what Spencer had disclosed to her boss at Jonah Stevens. She opted to live with the curiosity rather than ask.

Instead of a clinging Sheila, Spencer was with a sturdy, distinguished-looking gentleman, graying at the temples and dressed in an expensive suit. It appeared that they were business associates.

"Dinner for two?" she asked, reaching for menus.

Spencer managed a nod. He seemed preoccupied, and for some reason his disregard affected Marissa. She felt strangely disappointed.

Leading them to an oceanfront table, Marissa stepped aside, allowing them to take their seats. Her glances toward them, especially Spencer, were only of one dutifully waiting—until she noticed the stranger's watch. She stared in disbelief even after the watchband disappeared beneath his sleeve.

"I'm sorry," Marissa said, feigning embarrassment when the menus fell from her hands. "How clumsy of me."

She hesitated in her retrieval, allowing the man time to help. After he reached for the menus she quickly knelt and confirmed her initial glance. His watchband had the same etching as the one on Michael's pendant. Questions burned in her throat, but she couldn't ask him here, now, not knowing who he was or what she was up against. She quickly stood and, with a disarming smile, handed the stranger his menu and then gave Spencer his.

Marissa eyed Spencer uneasily, for his gaze seemed to indicate he had noticed the intentional mishap. She blinked away his insinuating stare as she recited the evening specials, maintaining a cool composure. "Enjoy your dinner," she finished.

The stranger nodded, unaware of her suspicions, and Marissa escaped to the podium, her heart beating much faster than the Musak playing in the background. If the etching was a duplicate, what about Gabe Hawkins only making originals? For some reason she believed the jeweler.

Back at the podium, she looked toward Spencer's table, wishing there were some way she could listen in on their conversation. Just to learn what the man's name was or what business he was in might provide a lead. When the cocktail waitress walked over to take their order, Marissa thought of an angle.

"There you are," Marissa said when she found Lynn in the pantry preparing dinner salads.

Lynn's hair had already begun slipping out from the many pins holding it back, and she moved her head with a practiced toss to get a strand out of her eyes. "Of course I'm here. You thought I'd deserted the ship?"

"Not on hula night," Marissa said with a chuckle. Saturday, after the hotel's well-known hula show, the restaurant flooded with tourists—most of them generous tippers. Rarely did a waitress give up the coveted evening. "We still have fifteen minutes before the crowd arrives," Marissa said. "I was wondering if you could do me a favor."

"Just as long as it isn't kissing the cook. I've had it with him tonight."

"I promise it's not. Come on over here." She led Lynn to a nearby bamboo divider. "See that man at table twelve sitting with Spencer?" Lynn peered between the bamboo poles and nodded. "He's wearing a watchband with an unusual etching. I was wondering if, being the charming waitress you are, you could subtly find out who he is and where he got the watch. The key word being subtle."

Lynn raised her eyebrows and said, "You want me to play spy?" Marissa nodded, hoping her request didn't sound too odd. "Can I ask why?"

"You can, but I won't tell you because it's—"

"It's for your research," Lynn said knowingly. "I'll give it a shot. You're going to let me read this book, aren't you?"

Marissa gave her friend a playful shrug. "I'll try to put some big spenders in your section tonight."

"What do you mean, tonight? You're supposed to do that every night," Lynn said, throwing back a smile as she went to deliver the salads.

"What did you find out?" Marissa asked Lynn nearly an hour later. They'd been terribly busy, but now the troop of hula guests were seated and enjoying their food.

"That he's an arrogant pig!" Lynn fumed. "When I asked about his watch, he just laughed and said, 'when you get into management, then we can talk.' "

"How rude."

"That's putting it politely," Lynn said, rolling her eyes. "Anyway, when I delivered their food, I overheard the guy ask Spencer for some special microphone. And later, they were talking about the King Kamehameha party."

"So you think this guy has some job at the party?"

Lynn shrugged. "Who cares. We, the lowly employees, never get invited. Only management."

A wry smile came to the corners of Marissa's mouth as she remembered John's invitation.

"Spencer called the guy Steve and—oh, I found this on the floor after they'd left." Lynn handed Marissa a glossy pamphlet.

Marissa read the bold letters "Power for Success" on the front and then scanned the verbiage inside. Something about it was familiar.

"Anything?" Lynn asked.

"Not really," Marissa said, slipping the pamphlet into her apron pocket. "Sounds interesting, though. I'll keep it just in—"

"Crowd control," Lynn interrupted, saying the words that had become a mutually understood signal that patrons were waiting.

Marissa gave Lynn a quick talk-to-you-later nod and headed for the podium. She mechanically played the role of pleasant hostess, but her heart wasn't in it. All she could think about was the pamphlet, its phony promises naggingly familiar. Could it possibly be a link to Michael's whereabouts?

After work, she ran up the steps to her condo, threw open the door, and started searching the kitchen table where she had piled up Michael's paper work. Her hands began to shake slightly when she found a similar pamphlet.

Without turning on the overhead paddle fan or taking off her blazer, Marissa sat down and began reading. The pamphlets boasted of a class that could change your life—rejuvenate you, bring you out of depression. Is that what Michael was feeling? Depression? Had he been that lonely? Michael's breakup with Lauren and their parents' deaths just weeks later had been a horrible combination for him. But normally he talked about his feelings. It wouldn't be like him to confide in strangers.

Of course, in the last few months Michael had been different. Nothing life changing; it was more subtle. She remembered a conversation they'd had one evening a few months ago.

"I didn't mean for it to be such a big deal," Michael said, rebuffed by her refusal to lend him money.

"It's not that I don't trust you," she said emphatically. "It's just that money deals always get so sticky, so personal. What do you need the money for, anyway?" They were eating dinner at Marissa's house. Michael had brought a pizza over and she had made a salad.

"I found this great investment, and I'm just a little short. Don't worry, I'll give you the money back . . . with interest."

"When did you get into investments, and what's 'a little short'?"

"Believe me, this is a good thing. A guy from New Covenant told me about it. He knows all about investing."

Marissa sighed. The very name New Covenant made her angry. "I don't know much about your new church, but I do know there can be cheaters anywhere . . . churches included."

Michael frowned, and she could almost feel another brick mortared between them. They had argued frequently the last few months, and suddenly Marissa wished she hadn't come down so hard on him. At least he'd been going to church somewhere.

"Okay, maybe I don't think much of your church because I miss not seeing you at ours," Marissa admitted. Michael nodded, appearing to accept her apology. "But tell me more about this investment. Who's it with?"

Michael slid a dark brown spiraled report across the table. "Here's their prospectus."

She paged through the booklet as he talked. "Ekvar?" she said. "Now that's a weird name. How much are you thinking of investing?"

"Twenty thousand."

Marissa nearly choked on her bite of pizza. "As in dollars?"

Michael nodded, avoiding her eyes as he reached for his soda. She sat there stunned. "I only need to borrow ten from you," he said.

"Only ten?" Her voice was sarcastic. "That's my half of Mom and Dad's cash account we just received."

"It's just a loan."

Marissa sighed again.

"I thought you'd be happy that I was doing something responsible with my money," Michael spat out.

"I am, it's just that . . ." Marissa paused, not wanting to say things she'd later regret.

"We're going to be getting the rest of Mom and Dad's inheritance any day, so you know I'm good for the money," Michael said.

"That lawyer has been promising he'll get us the money 'any day now' for months," Marissa retorted. "He sounds lazy to me."

"Uncle Hiram said he was sure it would be this month."

"Uncle Hiram is lazy *and* weird to boot," Marissa said. Michael didn't argue the point. As children they had concluded that their mother's brother was odd and not at all like their mom, who many times took him in after drinking binges. Then, quite suddenly, Hiram made a complete turnaround. He began working for another firm, bought a house, and even began sending his sister roses on her birthday again. He couldn't manage to salvage his marriage, but the rest of his life seemed to be going well. In his last Christmas card he'd written about a three-week vacation in the Bahamas.

"Whether it's one month or two, I'll pay you back with interest so it shouldn't matter to you," Michael stated firmly.

It shouldn't have, but somehow Michael's overnight zeal about investing didn't sit right with Marissa. Starting out with such a big amount and having to borrow to do it made her wary. But after a week of pestering, she gave in and handed Michael a check for ten thousand dollars, insisting he bring her additional paper work. He dropped off another report that didn't say much, but Marissa didn't feel like another argument and didn't pursue it further. And when they received the second lump of their inheritance money, Michael paid her back, assuring her that all was fine with him financially. Now she wished she had asked him more questions, saved the prospectus. But wishing wouldn't change anything now.

She picked up the pamphlet again, this time reading the small type on the back. *'Power for Success' seminars are not available to the general public. Classes are only offered to select private parties, professional groups, or by special invitation.*

"Wonderful," Marissa muttered. She didn't know enough people to form a group, much less a select one, and she doubted hostesses were leagued as professionals. Her only chance to learn more about the seminar, and perhaps the man with Spencer, would be by special invitation. Regretting saying no to John was a difficult admission; asking him to take her now, nearly impossible. Anyway, he already had a date, bribed and willing.

Marissa tapped her fingernails on the table, thinking. Then she stopped, her fingers in midair. Would she dare? She walked to her bedroom and paged through the clothes in her closet. Anything was worth a try.

Ten

Marissa smoothed the skirt of her sundress and held her head high as she walked through the door marked Regency Management Offices. Donald once told her she could sell the moon when she wore this particular dress. Today she merely hoped for a ticket to the King Kamehameha party.

A middle-aged receptionist with oversized glasses and hair pulled tautly back in a bun looked up. "Can I help you?"

"I'd like to speak with Spencer, if he's in," Marissa said.

"What's your business?"

"Personal. Spence asked that I stop by."

"Spence?" The receptionist repeated the casual title with disdain. "Mr. Mitchell's office is the last door on the right."

"Thank you," Marissa replied, relieved that she'd made it past the first obstacle.

Spencer's door was open. His sleeves were rolled up, his tie loosened around his neck, and he was studying a thick document. Marissa knocked softly on the door frame.

His initial look was warm, but an instant later it chilled. "If you're wondering about the security check, you passed."

"Yes, John told me. Thank you." She stood silent for a moment and then, foregoing her plan, said, "So you called Jonah Stevens?"

Spencer nodded.

"Did they ask where I was, what I was doing?"

"By 'they' do you mean Donald?"

Marissa stiffened, embarrassed that her intent was so transparent.

"Want to sit down?" Spencer motioned to one of the empty chairs in front of his mahogany desk. After an awkward silence, Marissa did.

"Donald did ask where you were," Spencer said, a smile hovering behind his lips, "but I said the position was confidential. He and I had an interesting chat, though. He said something about you quitting your job and running off without saying good-bye."

"I didn't quit my job," Marissa said evenly. "I'm using vacation days, and then I'll be on leave without pay."

"Still sounds like you broke his heart," Spencer observed, slightly amused.

"Did he mention he slept with his secretary?" Marissa blurted. She looked down an instant later, regretting the words. It was obvious Spencer was digging for information, and she had just unearthed a choice piece. But when she dragged her eyes back to his, the look of triumph she expected wasn't there. Instead there was quiet understanding.

"I thought there might be another side," he solemnly stated.

Marissa vacillated for a moment between confiding more to him or leaving the office out of embarrassment. Instead, she pulled a form from her purse. "I filled out the police report," she said, handing it to him.

Spencer examined the document for a moment, then looked back at her with questioning eyes. "Why the change of heart?"

She smoothed back an imaginary hair from her face. "I need a favor."

"A favor?" Spencer wrinkled his brow. "Like as in me doing something for you?" Marissa swallowed hard. "How about answering a question first—like why did you purposely drop the menus last Saturday night?"

Uncomfortable with the turn of tables, Marissa stood. Com-

ing here had been a shot in the dark anyway. "I'm sorry for taking up your time," she said. "Forget the favor."

"But you filled out the police report. Wouldn't it be a waste
if you didn't use it for something?" Spencer's voice had a sarcastic ring, but when he walked around to her side of the desk
a smile tugged at the corners of his mouth and he put out his
hand. "Truce?" he offered, looking her straight in the eyes.
"Despite everything, I think you must be a decent person."

"Thanks," she said, shaking his hand, "but I should have
filled out that form a long time ago."

"You're probably right, but now I'm curious. What was your
favor?"

Even with his proclamation of peace, she couldn't find it in
her to ask him. "It's okay. I shouldn't be asking you to do anything for me. You letting me keep my job is enough," she said,
turning toward the door.

"Let me make that decision," he quickly interjected. "What
do you need?"

Marissa turned back. He looked obliging, even willing. Was
she denying an opportunity to learn more about Michael? The
worst that could happen would be his turning her down.

Marissa licked her lips. "I heard that all managers get tickets
to the King Kamehameha party," she began. "I was wondering
if I could possibly buy a ticket from you, or if you could somehow allow me to attend."

A broad smile came to Spencer's face. "You're asking me for
a date?"

"A date?" Marissa's eyebrows rose suddenly. "No, you
don't understand. You don't need to accompany me. In fact, I'd
prefer to go alone."

Spencer assessed her features slowly, as if attempting to read
an unspoken message. "Oh . . . so you don't want to go with
me, you just want to go?"

Marissa nodded. However odd her request sounded, that's
exactly what she wanted.

Spencer leaned back and sat on the edge of his desk. "Rumor

has it they've already filled the guest list to overflowing and they aren't going to issue any more tickets." Marissa looked away, quick to accept defeat. Spencer continued, "I have two tickets, though, and I haven't asked anyone yet."

Marissa looked back, surprised. "But this is supposed to be *the* party of the year. I'm sure Sheila wouldn't want to miss out."

"She will, regardless. She's going to be out of town."

"Oh," Marissa said, unsure of exactly what the information meant.

"So I can take you, if you want. And if you went with me it would be a whole lot easier getting through the door."

"That would be nice—I mean . . . fine," Marissa said, stumbling over her words. There was something alluring about him, and she found it hard not to be thrilled to be his date—even if it really wasn't one.

A short beep sounded and a voice announced a waiting caller. "I'll talk to you next Saturday," Spencer said, his hand hovering over the phone. "We'll work out a time then."

Marissa's mouth twitched into a smile as she nodded her agreement, and with her heart pounding, she left the office.

❧   ❧   ❧   ❧

"It's love," Lynn concluded when Marissa arrived at the restaurant that evening.

"What are you talking about?"

"Flushed cheeks, extra energy. Did you meet someone at that snobbish little complex of yours?"

"No, and I'm not—"

"Going to," Lynn finished for her. "You never will with that attitude. Phil asked for your phone number again, so I gave it to him."

"You didn't!"

"You're right. But if you don't start dating, you'll never forget Donald and you'll eat yourself up with self-pity."

"Okay," Marissa said, "I'll say yes to the next decent guy who asks me out. Or better yet, I'll ask *him* out."

Lynn laughed. "Now that would be a leap in the right direction."

Eleven

A rusty pickup truck bumped along a deserted road flanked by fields of sugarcane, fine, red dust billowing behind it. Michael sat in the back with three others. Nobody talked. The sun was beating down hot on their heads, and the metal truck bed beneath them felt like a burner on high.

The lone woman looked like a throwback from the '60s. She sat with her legs crossed, her visage trancelike. The man next to her was a middle-aged Tongan, native to the islands of the southwest Pacific. He possessed a powerful build and dark skin mapped by scars and more than one tattoo. If he was there to keep them from leaping off the truck, it worked.

Next to Michael sat an elderly man. He coughed often, and several times he had reached into his shirt pocket and taken a few deep breaths from an inhaler. The fine dust wasn't doing him any favors.

"You okay?" Michael asked softly.

The man looked up, and for a second, there was a spark in his eyes. But just as quickly, it disappeared and he returned his stare out to the passing canes.

Michael looked over at the other two. The Tongan was nodding off to sleep, and the woman looked empty, like her soul had been transported to a different place. Maybe she thought it had. The tinted cab windows made it impossible to see if the driver was monitoring his passengers. They'd been ordered not to talk to one another, but Michael felt as if the old man knew something. He didn't look like one of "them." Besides, what would the driver do? He was already in the back of a dirty pickup, hungry and near dehydration.

"Know where we're going?" Michael whispered in a low voice.

The man continued staring, silent for a long while. "Do you like the heat?" he finally said. Michael studied the man for a moment and then put his head in his hands. A sprinkling of fine sand stuck to his palms. This man was as deranged as the rest of them. Michael couldn't remember the last time he'd had a normal conversation—like talking about work or who was going to win the play-offs.

The man spoke again. "Do you want your mind turned inside out until you don't know what's up or down?"

"No," Michael retorted. "I don't like the heat and I hate people who mess with my mind. This whole thing is insane." Anger lifted Michael's voice a few decibels. Delusionary or not, this old man was going to hear his story. "Some guys abduct me from my house and fly me here. No explanation. They take my money, try to brainwash me, and now they're driving me through some cane fields to—to what? Kill me? Heck, they're probably going to kill us all," Michael said, his voice even louder.

He'd reached his boiling point. Suddenly he stood up, wobbling horribly. "I've got a great idea," he roared. "Why don't you shoot me now. I'd be more useful as fertilizer for the fields than bumping around in the back of this miserable pickup."

The truck came to a ragged stop and the driver jumped out, holding a shotgun aimed at Michael. "Well," Michael shouted, hands outstretched, "what are you waiting for?" Exhausted, still sick with the flu, and in desperate need of water, Michael felt half-dead anyway.

"Sit down," a voice behind him commanded.

Michael turned toward the passenger side and saw Lee, dressed in a full suit, holding a leather attaché. "If it isn't Mr.

Abductor himself," Michael remarked, his voice drenched in sarcasm.

"Do you want another beating?" Lee said.

"Would you enjoy that?"

Lee remained motionless except for a nod to the Tongan, who was now fully awake and standing guard. "Teach him a lesson," Lee commanded.

Twenty minutes later Michael hobbled back to the truck. His face was bloody and his stomach hurt so badly that he had to stop and retch several times. When the truck jerked forward, Michael moaned and reached out for the old man's arm to steady himself. Something flickered around the man's neck and Michael focused on it. The pendant. Michael dropped the man's arm in disgust and clung to the hot truck instead. He'd been wrong about the old man. They were all his enemies.

Twelve

As Marissa dressed for the party, she whispered a prayer of thanks that her black dress had been in among the cluster of sundresses she'd hurriedly packed. Buying a dress for one night wasn't something she could afford. Neither were shoes. She looked at her only black pair with a frown and then back to her hair, attempting a French twist for the third time. She wanted to present an air of elegance. After all, Spencer was used to being with Sheila.

The doorbell rang at eight o'clock sharp. Marissa checked her lipstick in the hall mirror, inhaled deeply, then fumbled with the dead bolt in her attempt to open the door.

"What's with all the hardware?" Spencer asked with a crooked smile. "Sounded like you were unlocking a vault."

"Just a stubborn dead bolt." Marissa motioned him in, trying not to notice how handsome his blue eyes were or how his athletic body moved in his black tuxedo.

"By the way, you look great," he commented, appearing relaxed and comfortable.

Absorbed in the warmth of his eyes, Marissa hoped her voice wouldn't betray her nervousness. "Thank you. You look nice yourself."

Spencer walked into the living room and looked up. "So you have the floor plan with the loft. That really makes it spacious."

Marissa couldn't think of an intelligent reply. She felt like a teenager on prom night. "I just have to get my purse," she said, darting toward the bedroom. "There's coffee in the kitchen," she called over her shoulder, her voice trailing off as she walked down the hall.

This isn't smart, she told herself as she escaped into the bedroom and leaned against the cool wall, her heart pounding. *Don't you dare think about romance. Sure, the guy's cute. Well, more than cute. Drop-dead gorgeous. But he has a girlfriend and you have to find some connection to Michael tonight. Who knows, Spencer might even be connected to the enemy. Don't share anything personal tonight—not one thing.* Pep talk given and purse retrieved, Marissa walked back to the living room.

Spencer was holding a coffee cup, looking at the photograph she had taken from Michael's apartment. "Your boyfriend?" he asked.

"Brother," she answered automatically, inwardly chastising herself for not saying yes. How many pep talks would she have to give herself tonight?

"Nice house," Spencer commented, motioning to her parents' estate sprawled behind them in the photo. "Don't tell me it's yours."

"I won't," she answered lightheartedly. Touché. Now that wasn't hard. But she didn't expect Spencer's next words.

"Another personal question. Sorry." Spencer set the framed photo back on top of the TV. "I'll try to stay away from those tonight."

He's smooth, Marissa thought as she turned off the coffee maker and locked the door behind them. Smooth and handsome—a dangerous combination.

"I snapped her up," Spencer said as they walked down the outdoor staircase toward his red convertible. "I didn't think you'd like the wind messing up your hair."

"Sounds like that's been suggested to you before," Marissa noted, thinking of Sheila and her demands on him.

"Yeah, by my mom. She was my first passenger."

Surprised and for some reason happy over his answer, Marissa asked, "Does your mom live on the island?"

Spencer shook his head. "Colorado. But she visits a couple times a year. She stayed with me for six months after Dad died. It gave her time away from the house—they lived there for thirty-eight years." As Spencer opened the passenger door he added, "Looks like you're going to learn a lot about me tonight, and me, hardly anything about you."

"I'll tell you one thing about *my* mother," Marissa said, hesitating before getting in the car. "She told me not to go anywhere with a stranger."

Spencer held her eyes for a moment. "I was sort of hoping we were beyond that."

The party was glitzy, and wealth—real or rented—was flaunted. As Spencer and Marissa made their way through the hotel's foyer and out to the terrace, a woman decked out in diamonds and wearing a flamboyant dress strode up, demanding their attention. Marissa recognized her instantly. Sheila's mother.

"Sheila must be out of town." The haughty tone dared to be challenged.

"She is," Spencer said matter-of-factly. "Marissa Tomsen, this is Gladys Day. Gladys and her husband own the Club Bay Vista."

Marissa smiled, impressed at how well Spencer held his composure.

"And what is your relationship to Spencer?" Gladys said, looking pointedly at Marissa. Was it only her imagination, or had Gladys already noted her scuffed shoes?

"I'm his neighbor," Marissa said with forced optimism.

"How sweet of you to invite your neighbor," Gladys told Spencer in mocking sincerity. "I hope Sheila has a neighbor with her tonight, too." Flinging a final cool appraisal, she walked away.

Marissa cringed as she looked over at Spencer, but he didn't appear to be concerned with the situation. He picked up two glasses of punch from the tray of a proffering waiter and handed her one.

"Sorry for the interrogation," he said. "I'm used to that wonderful woman, but I don't suppose you are." His blue eyes were playful and yet sad, as though he regretted the strained relationship.

"You deserve a medal for patience," Marissa stated.

"No," he said, nodding at someone he knew and then looking back to Marissa. "Her husband does."

Several friends came up and slapped Spencer on the back. He introduced Marissa and they bantered easily. Spencer was so unlike Donald, who flaunted his position whenever possible, and she had to smile when Spencer introduced himself to a newly appointed Kihei hotel manager as "a gopher for the Regency."

"Hope you didn't eat dinner," Spencer said as he guided her to the tables loaded with platters of choice seafood, tropical fruits, aged cheeses, tantalizing meats, assorted breads, and mouth-watering desserts. He handed Marissa a plate, taking one for himself.

After choosing all they wanted, they found a linen-topped table for two near the enormous pool, and Spencer took off his jacket and draped it across the back of his chair. Marissa couldn't help but notice how his crisp white shirt and black cummerbund lay taut across his lean, muscular stomach, and she had to force her eyes to her plate so he wouldn't catch her stare.

"How long have you been with the Regency?" she asked, trying to think of him as she would a client with Jonah Stevens.

"Four years going on thirty," Spencer said with a sigh. "I can't complain, though. They pay me well enough."

"But there's something else you'd rather be doing?"

Spencer nodded as if recalling a wonderful thought. "Flying."

"As in a fighter jet or a small airplane?"

Spencer chuckled. "I've never flown a fighter. But I can handle small planes pretty well, and helicopters. A friend and I own a Jet Ranger. I moonlight on my days off. Most times my passengers are crates of bottled water and boxes of T-shirts, but occasionally I get to take up a sightseer or two."

"So you want to start a flight-seeing business?" Marissa said, enthralled with the idea.

"You make it sound so easy."

"Seems to me it would be. You've probably saved up some big bucks with a hotel manager's salary, and you know lots of people in the tourist industry. Of course, I'm sure you've thought of all this yourself."

A grin tugged at the corner of his mouth. "It sounds good on paper. I just don't have the guts to quit my job. Too dependent on that paycheck every other week, I guess. With a business of my own, I may be lucky to eat shaved ice for the first few months, if not years."

"Then open two businesses," Marissa teased, suddenly feeling lighthearted.

Spencer raised his eyebrows inquisitively. "Two?"

"Yeah. A flight-seeing business and a shaved ice stand. At least then you could eat for free."

Spencer chuckled. "Thanks for the vote of confidence."

"No, really," she said, turning serious. "I think you should go for it. If you don't, you'll probably always wish that you had."

"You sound like my brother," Spencer said. "He has more guts than I do. He quit his job and moved to Australia. He and his wife operate a trading store there. They don't make much money, but they're happy."

"Have you been there—to Australia, I mean?"

"Fritz keeps inviting me, but whenever I make plans to go, some crisis comes up at work and I have to cancel."

Music drifted over from the live band. Spencer looked toward the large hardwood platform and then back to Marissa. "Want to dance?"

"We don't have to," she heard herself say.

"I know." Spencer stood and held out his hand. "I want to."

Marissa was acutely aware of the warmth that crept over her body as she stared up into his inviting blue eyes. She wanted to offer him a polite no—but instead, she offered her hand.

He led her to the dance floor and held her in a light embrace. His neatly pressed shirt smelled fresh and clean, and his body felt like a strong, safe wall. As she gazed over his shoulder a gamut of emotions washed over her. If only she could stay here in Spencer's arms, with the firelight from the many torches reflecting off the clear water, the slow song suggesting romance. But tonight was just an interlude and maybe not even that. The evening could end much differently. The beat quickened, and two songs later they returned to their table.

"You're a good dancer," Marissa observed with a smile.

"I try not to make a fool of myself dancing or drinking," Spencer replied.

Marissa was relieved. She'd had no idea how Spencer was going to conduct himself tonight, and she'd been happily surprised when he'd declined the cocktail waitress the first time she came by and then again now. She waited, thinking that he would share his reason for nixing alcohol, but he didn't and a silence hung between them.

"Well," Spencer said after a moment, "was there something special you wanted to do, or was it the Hawaiian meatballs you were after?"

Marissa smiled. Three small meatballs were the only appetizer left on her plate. "Too greasy," she said apologetically and then paused, her smile fading. "I saw a poster when we first walked in. Something about a 'Power for Success' seminar. It's to be held in the banquet room, and I thought I could maybe listen in."

Spencer's eyebrows rose. "You're interested in a phony seminar?"

"Phony? Isn't the presenter your friend?"

"You mean Steve Porter?"

Marissa nodded.

"A business dinner doesn't mean we're friends. I'm in no way supportive of his New Age seminars."

"Is that what they are?"

"Just a wild guess. Are you a New Ager?" He looked at her as though her answer meant a great deal to him.

"No," Marissa said. "I just thought the presentation might be interesting."

A slight disappointment clouded his eyes and he glanced across the terrace. "If that's what you came for we better head on over. Looks like people are gathering there."

His voice was unenthusiastic, and Marissa thought it odd that he would offer to accompany her to something he apparently didn't approve of, but she didn't say anything. She wasn't about to jeopardize what could be a lead to Michael.

Marissa and Spencer accepted brochures from a young woman at the door, then walked in and found seats near the middle of the fast-filling banquet room. Marissa read the paper work with interest. Spencer didn't bother. Minutes later an energetic and looking-as-though-he-loved-what-he-did-for-a-living Steve Porter waltzed to the front. His tailored suit and silk tie evidenced success, and his hair was peppered with just enough gray to authenticate experience.

"I am honored to be here tonight," Steve proclaimed, clearly at ease with being in front of an audience. "And I'm not just saying that. I'm knocked-off-my-socks happy to get to rub elbows with you—the elite of this paradise island. Just look at you," he said, gracefully removing the microphone from its stand and walking toward an elderly woman. "Wow," he said, gently picking up her hand. Then he whistled low. "Now *this* is a diamond."

The woman smiled, unable to hide her pride over the atrociously large rock. Steve gave her hand a friendly squeeze and walked farther down the aisle, acknowledging other displays of affluence. "You are successful people," he said. "One way or another, you've made it to the top." Then he stopped and put a hand to his forehead. "So why are you here? Don't you know I teach a course on success?" He looked around with a bemused expression as faint laughter echoed across the room.

With energetic steps, he made his way back to the podium. "I hope it's because you want to be even better. Inside and out. You've made the money . . . now you can claim your inner peace, your inner harmony—the real you. Now," he paused, "you Christians out there, don't worry. My grandmother raised me, and the Bible was the number one book in our house. I appreciated having guidelines. Well, actually not until I got older—the end of her cane hurt." Faint laughter again.

"But we do need to balance the body, mind, and emotions. Thomas Rooka, the man who wrote this seminar's material, has spent ten years listening, learning, working, and focusing on reducing stress and getting more of those mountain-top experiences. You know, those personal moments when you're struck by a beautiful sunset, or when a relationship deepens, or when someone thanks you just for being there. After taking this course, I was a changed person, and now I feel compelled to share it with you."

Steve's voice was authoritative and extremely convincing. Most of what he was saying was interspersed with common sense. Eerily, Marissa remembered Michael telling her some of the same concepts—as if he'd heard the ideas several times. When Steve concluded, he made a flawless transition into inviting those interested to sign up for the upcoming seminar, and as he glided off the stage several people were already walking forward.

"So what do you think?" Spencer asked.

"I guess I came for the meatballs after all," Marissa said with a half smile.

"Good," Spencer said, standing. "Let's get out of here."

As they weaved their way in between chairs to reach the aisle to exit, Marissa looked toward the people gathered around the sign-up table. Was she forfeiting an opportunity to find Michael? Wasn't this the reason she came?

"Spencer, I need to use the ladies' room," Marissa said, glancing toward a rest room sign off to the right. "How about if I meet you back by the fountain in a few minutes?" He nodded agreeably and they went their separate ways.

Emerging from the rest room less than a minute later, Marissa doubled back to the banquet hall. Every fiber in her body detested the thought of involving herself with this organization, but she would do it—for Michael.

"I'd like to sign up for your next session," Marissa told Steve when she approached the front of the line.

Steve's smile widened and his deep-set eyes held hers invitingly. "You won't be disappointed," he told her in a voice just as smooth as it had been over the microphone. "I've promoted many courses and this is by far the best." He handed her a pen and a registration form and then busied himself with another applicant. Relieved that he hadn't recognized her as the hostess from the Regency, Marissa wrote her name and telephone number, hesitated on the address, and ended up writing down the hotel's. She drew a sharp breath at the last paragraph which listed the exorbitant fee. The following sentence suggested asking an employer for compensation and went on to list many Fortune 500 companies already subsidizing the course. Corporate approval for such a course didn't sit right with Marissa. Nothing about this course felt right.

Steve looked pleased when she handed back the form. "Here's directions to the office suite," he said, giving her a small envelope. "We'll see you at the first session, Miss—" he paused to read her name off the form. For a fraction of a second, Marissa saw recognition flash across his face, followed by a horrible, dark expression. But it vanished just as quickly. "Miss Tomsen," he finished. "Yes, we'll see you then." The smile didn't match his mercurial eyes that sent a warning dagger through her very core.

Thirteen

Trembling, Marissa walked out of the banquet room and excused her way through the crush of people on the terrace. Steve had recognized her last name. His eyes betrayed him. She wanted to run back and demand that he tell her where Michael was. But he would probably only shrug and, with a phony smile, tell her he didn't know who she was talking about.

Suddenly a dark-suited arm reached out for her. Gasping, she jerked away, jarring a nearby couple.

"Marissa, it's me," she heard a familiar voice say.

Marissa looked around to see Spencer. In her haste to distance herself from Steve Porter, she had walked right past him.

Spencer apologized to the nearby couple and led Marissa to the other side of the fountain. "Is everything okay? You're trembling." Spencer looked at her intently, his clear blue eyes serious.

"I'm just a little cold, that's all." There was a slight breeze, and with her sleeveless dress, the excuse was believable.

"Here, put on my coat," he offered, slipping his jacket around her shoulders. His concern touched her heart and she wanted to cling to him as Sheila had done on the elevator. Instead, she pulled the jacket tight around her and rubbed her arms.

"This is about the time I leave, anyway," Spencer said, leading her past the packed dance floor and the long lines leading to the food tables. They took a smaller side corridor that was less crowded.

"I hope I'm not taking you away from people you need to be mingling with," Marissa said, trying to be diplomatic and yet at the same time feeling relieved that Steve Porter was becoming more distant with each step.

"Oh, there is one person I need to talk with," Spencer said, stopping suddenly. "Do you mind waiting? It shouldn't take long." Marissa had no desire to be in the hotel for one minute longer, but she politely agreed and watched as Spencer walked back down the hall and turned the corner.

The auxiliary hallway was spacious and the art cheerful, yet the lights were dim and with no one around, Marissa began to feel anxious. The more time passed, the more fears she dredged up. What if Steve were to wander down this hallway? Worse yet, what if he was looking for her? She was alone in a hallway with only one exit. . . .

Stepping into the shadow of a mammoth archway, Marissa looked toward the wide open foyer and then back down the hall again. Steve's demeanor continued to disturb her, and she wondered how she was ever going to capture enough courage to attend the "Power for Success" classes. But she had to go. She sensed that Steve knew about Michael.

Another glance down the hall caused Marissa to stiffen. Her fear of seeing Steve materialized. Still hidden in the shadows, Marissa watched him walk across the lobby and then pause next to a distant cascading waterfall. He appeared to be talking to someone out of her line of vision, and she had no desire to step out of the shadow and check who. He used his hands several times as if for emphasis, then strode back toward the pool area, defiance punctuating his movements. Marissa let out a sigh of relief when he was out of sight.

Spencer returned a moment later, hailed a valet, and soon they were in his car heading home. "Sorry again for the wait," Spencer said, following the car ahead of him too closely and then having to brake suddenly.

"Can't get away from business, huh?"

"Always seems that way," he muttered, squinting at the on-coming headlight glare. He seemed different somehow, as if he'd argued with someone and was still upset.

"What was the problem tonight?" Marissa prodded.

"Just something to do with the microphones."

Suddenly Marissa connected Spencer's changed mood with her witness of Steve. Could Spencer have been the one Steve was arguing with? "Steve's?" Marissa asked with growing uneasiness.

Spencer acted surprised. "Yeah. Why?"

"Nothing. I just guessed." Marissa's throat tightened as she stared into the blackness, wanting nothing more than to get home.

"You seem on edge."

"I'm fine, really." She tried to sound light and casual.

Spencer shrugged and let it go. They drove in silence for a few minutes and then, quite suddenly, Spencer turned off the highway onto a side road. "I want to show you a favorite beach. It's back here a ways—kind of hidden."

Fear swept Marissa's body. A secluded beach . . . Spencer just having talked with Steve . . . Spencer must be one of them. What did they intend to do with her? Marissa slowly moved her hand toward the door handle. She would put up a struggle. She would not go like a lamb to the slaughter.

As they drove over the uneven ground, Spencer slowed the car. Marissa held the handle tightly now. A little slower and she could do it. As Spencer neared a sandy knoll, she picked her moment and lunged out of the car.

"Marissa!" she heard Spencer shout.

Jerking off her shoes, she half ran, half slid down the sandy embankment. A moment later she heard another car pull up. Voices, doors slamming, shadows clamoring down the slope after her—she'd escaped just in time. Her heart pounded hard, as much from fear as her physical efforts to run on the loose sand.

Like a small boat with a tidal wave approaching, she felt an ominous power behind her.

Reaching the firm, damp sand, her run turned into a sprint. Sucking air in and out, arms close to her side, she used every bit of energy to widen the gap between her and her pursuer. Steve Porter's face flashed in her mind. The contemptuous eyes, the plastic smile. What had he done to Michael? What would happen to her? Glancing over her shoulder, she saw two shadows. Bigger, but slower.

Lungs on fire and waves lapping at her feet, she made out lights and the silhouette of trees and then a condominium complex twenty yards off to her right. She would be safe there. Knowing her speed would slow considerably on the loose sand, she chose to run until she was even with the building and then turn inland. She pushed herself hard on the soft sand.

Nearly to the trees, her ankle struck hard against a rusty anchor embedded in the sand and she tripped. Pain radiated up her leg, bringing tears to her eyes. Grimacing, she crawled to her knees and looked behind. The shadowy forms were easier to make out, and soon they would be closing in on her. Ignoring the burning sensation from her ankle, she scrambled to her feet and darted behind a towering palm tree. Leaning against it, breathing heavily, she looked toward the light. A few more yards and she would reach the complex.

But a second later an arm caught her around the waist and a hand covered her mouth. She bit down hard but only tasted a leather object covering her attacker's hand. Held tightly, she was half carried, half dragged behind a clump of monstera plants. Marissa struggled hard when she saw the shadows of her pursuers approaching from the beach. She fully expected her attacker to signal to his partners that he'd found her, but he remained silent, holding her in a vise-like grip. The shadows, now having turned into real people, ran past and then tried to walk inconspicuously across the complex grounds. After a moment there were voices, car doors slamming, a motor accelerating, and then silence.

"I think they're gone," the voice behind her whispered.

Released, Marissa spun around, ready to run—only to see Spencer. The sleeve of his tux was torn, his tie missing, and he was wiping perspiration off his forehead. Marissa's eyes raked his face with a mixture of surprise and relief. Then she looked behind her and past Spencer's shoulder, still hesitant to believe the chase was over.

"How did you get here?" she said softly, her heart still pounding in her throat. "And . . . and what were you doing back there?"

"What was *I* doing back there?" Spencer said. "I *was* going to show you one of my favorite beaches. Then you run off like I'm some serial killer. A second later some guys pull up like they're on assignment with the FBI and start chasing you."

"Who were they?" Marissa asked guardedly, rubbing her arms that ached from where he had held her.

"Oh, come on," Spencer said. "Your boyfriend pleaded with me to tell him where you were. He's rich and jealous. You figure it out."

"Donald hired someone to follow me?"

"Was your boyfriend before Donald the jealous type, too?"

She gave him a cold stare.

"Sorry," he said, brushing sand off his clothes. "I guess you've been through enough tonight." In the glow of the grounds' lights, she saw one of her shoes with teeth marks in the leather and realized that that was what she had bitten into. She and Sheila's mom would be in agreement over their demise, she thought wryly, wincing from the stinging of her ankle as she moved her foot.

"I took a shortcut through the trees and came out just as you fell," Spencer said, leaning down to inspect her injury. "Did you hit a rock or something?"

"A rusty anchor."

"Yeow," Spencer said. "How bad is it?"

"It hurts, but I can walk with it."

"It's pretty much caked with blood and sand. Not a great

mix, but good enough until we can get back to the condo." Spencer rose cautiously, surveying the area.

"Do you see anyone?" Marissa's voice was anxious.

"Looks clear to me," Spencer said.

"I'm sorry for all of this," Marissa apologized as they made their way through the trees. "I'll pay for your tux and anything else that was ruined."

"Only if you send Donald the bill," Spencer retorted with a look of disdain.

Even though Marissa felt certain her pursuer wasn't Donald, she wasn't going to argue. She had survived the chase. That's all she could consider right now.

When they returned to her condo, Marissa headed to the kitchen. "There's a first-aid kit under here somewhere," she said, kneeling down to look underneath the kitchen sink. "Here it is." She pulled the box out and slid it across the counter toward Spencer.

"Now *this* is a first-aid kit," Spencer commented after opening the three-tiered metal box. "Syringes, IVs, sutures . . . I feel like operating."

"The man who arranged for me to stay here is a doctor," Marissa said, walking to the couch. She propped her leg up on the coffee table, wincing as she pressed a damp dishcloth against her ankle.

"Maybe that's what made Donald mad—you dating a doctor." Spencer carried the kit and deposited it on the table.

"The doctor is seventy-four years old," Marissa said with a small smile. "He and his wife are almost like parents to me. They knew I needed a place to stay for a while."

"So you're only going to be on the island for a few weeks?" Spencer asked, sitting beside her and watching her clean the sand off her leg.

Marissa kept her eyes on the wound and her movements became slower as she considered what to tell him.

"Guess you're going to hold to your code of silence, huh?" he concluded.

Marissa looked up sharply, surprised at his choice of words. He shrugged his shoulders as if waiting for her reply. Hadn't he helped her? Didn't he have a right to know who was after them tonight? Yet despite his kindness, something stopped her from telling him her situation.

"I appreciate what you did for me tonight," she began, "but I honestly don't know how long I'll be here."

"Then that means when you know, you'll tell me?"

She nodded, liking the way his eyes softened and wishing more than ever she were just there on a tropical vacation.

"Sounds fair." He handed her some gauze and a tube of antiseptic.

Once her bandage was in place, Marissa insisted on making some coffee. As she offered a mug to him, she caught her reflection in the dining room mirror and moaned. "I look—"

"Great," he finished for her.

"Right," Marissa scoffed, staring in the mirror. "My hair is a mess, my shoulder strap is broken, I'm coated with sand, and my shoes have teeth marks on them." Exasperated, she tucked some hair back in her twist only to have it fall back to her shoulder. Then she looked over at Spencer. His disheveled appearance didn't look much better, and when their eyes met, they suddenly both broke out laughing.

"I've gone to six King K parties," Spencer said, still chuckling, "and this one was by far the most entertaining. Were you ever in track and field? You set a mean pace."

"High school," Marissa said with a smile as she walked back to the living room and elevated her ankle in an extended easy chair. "I still have a few blue ribbons, I think."

Spencer returned the smile, then became serious. "Why did you run in the first place?"

"I guess I let my imagination get the best of me," Marissa said, trying to act nonchalant as she pulled one of Myrtle's handmade quilts off the back of the chair and wrapped it around her. "Temporary insanity, I guess. I'm sorry."

A silence fell between them. "I better let you get some

sleep." Spencer observed her relaxed form. "You look comfortable, so don't bother getting up . . . I'll let myself out. Good night."

"Good night," she answered back softly.

After the door clicked shut, Marissa let her head sink back against the chair. Despite the terror she had felt tonight, her thoughts lingered on Spencer—the way he talked, how his eyes held hers, the way he'd helped her. She wondered if he was thinking about her, too. Of course, his thoughts about her could be totally different since she wasn't willing to confide in him and he knew she'd had a stormy relationship in the past. Maybe he was thinking that he didn't want anything to do with her.

Suddenly the telephone's ring shattered the silence. Marissa's heart leapt and began beating an erratic rhythm. It was three in the morning. Was Steve already making a move? Cautiously, she whispered a soft hello into the receiver.

"Sorry if I scared you." It was Spencer's familiar voice. "I just didn't want you falling asleep before you turned that dead bolt. There's crime everywhere, you know."

A chill went through Marissa after she hung up. Had Spencer already determined that the chase was about more than jealousy?

Fourteen

The resort was large and rustic. The woman and elderly man climbed out of the truck and walked toward the front entrance. Michael was escorted by the Tongan guard to the rear entrance and down a steep stairway to a long, narrow room furnished with a simple bed, desk, and a chair. "You make noise, you get another beating," the guard said, putting a cassette into a tape player on the far wall and then locking a lid over it with a key.

Michael was in no condition to argue. All he wanted was to lie down, or maybe throw up and then lie down. After the guard left and the lock clicked into place, the voice on the tape began. "Your destiny is of your choosing. . . . Reality is what you make. . . . Claim the inner you. . . . Truth changes as your understanding changes."

"Yeah, I'll just visualize myself back home," Michael said to the bare walls. "Or should I click my heels together?"

Enraged over their continued attempts at brainwashing, Michael limped around the room, his battered body crying out in protest as he tried the door and searched for speaker wires. When he bent to check under the desk, a wave of nausea swept over him and he hurried toward the only other door in the room. He threw up in the toilet and then scrubbed his hands and face at the airline-sized sink. There was no soap, but the cool water felt good.

Putting off his search for the speaker wires, he lay down on the bed. He needed rest, not another beating. The tape told him to relax and think of himself floating. No one mattered but himself. He was ruler. Everything was up to him. He drifted in and out of troubled sleep.

❦   ❦   ❦   ❦

"Get up if you want to eat," the Tongan said, giving Michael a rough nudge with his boot. Michael opened his eyes, stiffly stood, and followed his impatient guide down the hall. Handing him a bundle of clothes, the guard motioned toward a door. "I'll wait ten minutes," he said gruffly.

Michael pushed open the door and found a community bathroom—four toilet stalls, showers, two rows of lockers, no windows, and no other doors. His rubber-soled shoes squeaked on the tile floor. He quickly removed them and spent his first two precious minutes searching lockers. Most were padlocked or empty, but he managed to find a wire hanger. Maybe he could use it to pick the lock of his room and get out of this place. He hid it under the bundle of clothes.

Now for an overdue shower. Pulling off his shirt, he caught his reflection in a mirror. A thinner man with beard stubble on his face and a bruised lower lip stared back at him. He felt humiliated over his choices these last few months and angry that someone would use his weakness for their gain. Turning away from the mirror, he finished undressing and tried to appreciate the refreshing stream of warm water and the small piece of soap he'd found in one of the trays.

Hurriedly, he dried off with paper toweling and put on the clothes the guard had given him. The white cotton boat-necked shirt was torn, and it had a large number 6 written on both the front and back. Michael had no idea what the number meant. The pants were too short, but they were clean, as were the white socks and too big white sneakers. Just as he finished rolling his jeans and shirt around the hanger, the guard pushed the door open. Michael felt him eye the bundle, but he only nodded him back to the hallway and up a stairway.

"Meet me back here at twelve-thirty," the guard told him when they arrived at the cafeteria door. "You can only eat outside at the far table. No talking. If you don't follow the rules, I'll forget to bring you here. Understand?" Michael nodded and the man walked away.

Already salivating at the thought of food, Michael tucked his clothes under one arm and picked up a tray. He glanced at the men and women talking and eating at the tables. They, too, wore the same white clothing except theirs didn't have a number. Some were deep in conversation, some laughing—they didn't appear to be held against their will.

A bald man ahead of him in line glanced back, looked at his number, then smiled broadly. "I want you to know that I'm proud of you for trying to make a go of your life."

Michael looked blankly at the man and didn't say anything. Maybe this was a test, and he didn't want to lose his eating privileges.

"It's okay," the man continued, "all of us get messed up once in a while. It sure is nice this resort hires ex-convicts like you. I know it would be tough getting a job after . . . you know, after having a record. Well, anyway, I've been meaning to encourage you guys. If you see the other guy, tell him what I said, huh?"

Michael nodded weakly as the well-meaning bald man continued down the line. There was another man in his same position? A victim like himself, or really an ex-con? Apparently this vindictive group had an explanation for everything they did.

"Tofu or chicken?" the man behind the counter asked.

"Chicken," Michael said. He was served a small portion of meat, rice, and a vegetable he'd never seen before. Reaching toward a basket of fruit, Michael glanced ahead to the end of the line. A tall woman with long black hair was perched on a stool, staring at him with dark, penetrating eyes. He felt uncomfortable and looked away.

"Mike Tomsen?" she said, her lips twisting into a smile.

Michael took a glance her way, put two oranges on his tray, and continued down the line, regretfully toward her.

"Welcome to Tropical Dreams Resort," she said when he reached her. "These are vitamins," she said, handing him a paper cup half full with a red liquid. "We suggest you take them right away so you won't forget."

Something convinced him that nothing she gave him would be good. "Oh, I'll be sure to take them." Michael set the cup on his tray, eager to walk past her and having no intention of drinking the contents.

"No," the woman said, putting a hand on his arm, "I'll be sure." She picked the cup back up and held it out to him.

"You're forcing me?"

She produced a synthetic smile. "We want you to be healthy."

"I have my doubts."

"Derrick," the woman said softly but firmly, not taking her eyes off Michael. The familiar hulk appeared and stood behind the woman.

"An example of how potent the vitamins are?" Michael asked sarcastically. But he drank the bitter liquid anyway, having learned his lesson on disobedience yesterday.

Fifteen

I used to get my hair done and my nails manicured at least once a month," Lynn told Marissa as she peered into the small mirror attached to her locker door. "Now my nails are never even polished, and to save money, I go to a beauty school for haircuts. They do a terrible job."

Lynn's comment and the displeasure in her expression gave Marissa an idea, and the next day during their dinner break, she led Lynn into the women's lounge.

"What's up?" Lynn asked.

"You'll see," Marissa said with a grin, directing Lynn to a chair she'd pulled over next to the sink. Opening her tote, Marissa pulled out two towels, some hair products, a comb, and a pair of scissors. "I know you're short on time and money, so I thought I'd offer my services." She handed Lynn two magazine pictures. "You choose the style. I think you'd look great in either one."

"You can really cut hair?" Lynn said, surprised.

"I learned from a roommate in college." Marissa began wrapping a towel around Lynn's shoulders. "And don't worry, I didn't get many complaints."

Lynn chuckled, obviously happy with the offer. "I don't complain about anything that's free."

"Free? I never said that."

"If you want my tips for the evening, you're dreaming,"

Lynn teased as Marissa motioned for her to lean her head back over the sink. "Say, Marcy said she's subbing a few hours for you on Wednesday and Saturday nights. Need more time to write?"

"I do, but I can't afford it. I'm taking a class for a few weeks. Hopefully it will help my writing . . . we'll see. Now cover your eyes," Marissa said, "this sink was not designed for this." Marissa talked about different hairstyles then, thankful she had the excuse to change the subject. Finally she directed the conversation to one Lynn would be stuck on indefinitely—John.

"Heard anything about the boss lately?"

"Oh, forgot to tell you," Lynn said. "I overheard John and Spencer talking. Guess John's wife finally got smart. She's divorcing him." Marissa nodded. It had only been a matter of time. "After John's sob story, Spencer started asking about you."

"What about?" Marissa said, hoping she didn't sound too interested.

"Oh, like what your schedule was. Stuff like that. Sounded like he wanted to ask you out on a date."

"I thought he had a girlfriend."

"Sheila?"

"You know her?"

"Word gets out. Especially when the boss is cute." Lynn chuckled. "I hear she's a flight attendant and that she's out of town a lot. He probably gets lonesome when she's gone."

"You are horrible," Marissa said, swatting Lynn with a towel. "For that, you'll get the shorter style."

"No way. I still want the longer one."

"Chicken."

Thirty minutes later, a younger-looking, more professional Lynn looked at her reflection in the mirror. "I really appreciate you doing this," Lynn said, eyeing her new chin-length bob, slightly layered near her face and softly curled under. "I love it. Maybe my kids will even notice me tonight." She looked back to Marissa, who was busily putting the hair dryer, curling iron, scissors, and bottles back into her bag. "How did you carry all that?"

"It was heavy. You're driving me home."

Lynn laughed. "It's a deal."

❦   ❦   ❦   ❦

Marissa waited impatiently in line for a rental car. The small office was packed, mainly with tourists anxious to pick up their vehicles and get on with their vacations. In line in front of her, two tow-headed boys scuffled while their parents questioned the salesperson as if she were the Maui Visitor Bureau.

Marissa wished she didn't have to spend money on a car, but she had checked the bus schedule and there was no service out as far as the seminar building when the "Power for Success" class ended. She would just have to bear one more expense.

"I need a small, compact car," she told the balding man behind the counter when she finally made it to the front. "Your least expensive one." He typed some information into a computer, and after the printer spit out the paper work, he laid a set of keys on the counter and pointed to where she should sign. For the first time in her life she didn't know if she'd have enough money to cover the bill when it arrived. Being in a hurry gave her little time to dwell on the situation; besides, she knew worrying would do her no good.

She drove home and hurried up the steps to her condo, noting she still had a few minutes to spare. Picking up the phone, she dialed the Thibedeauxes' familiar number. "Collect, please," she told the operator, following through on Ernest and Myrtle's request that she call them once a week.

Pessimism could have easily drenched the conversations, since nothing of certainty had surfaced on either end; but each time, Myrtle was quick to offer a secure hope. "Do you have a pen handy?" she would ask near the end of the call. "I have another Bible verse for you." Today's verse was Jeremiah 29:11.

"Got it," Marissa said, and after she hung up, she flipped to

Jeremiah in her Bible and copied the words on an index card. With Myrtle's encouragement, she was memorizing Scripture again. Throughout the day, verses would come to her mind, refreshing and strengthening her like waters of renewal. How she needed to meditate on God's Word. She would prop the card up in the car and memorize it on the way.

Locking her condo, she quickly walked down the exterior flight of steps, then paused when she noticed Sheila perched on Spencer's car. The self-assured beauty was wearing a silk tank top, sarong skirt, and an even more elaborate diamond necklace around her tanned neck. Marissa wondered if Spencer had given it to her to replace the one she'd lost on the elevator.

When Spencer's condo door opened and he appeared, Marissa ducked behind a lattice divider.

"Take me to dinner, you handsome hunk," she heard Sheila say.

"You're back a day early." A smile warmed his face. Marissa felt foolish spying on them between the slates in the lattice. She should have just said hello and walked on by. But now there was no way to leave without exposing her inane action, so she remained, a prisoner of her own doing.

Spencer gave Sheila a swift kiss, but she was reluctant to let him go and pressed her lithe body against his. "I'm in town for five days, and I want to see you every minute."

Spencer laughed. "My meetings this week are very boring. You wouldn't like them."

"I wish I worked in town," she pouted. "I never get to see you."

"Oh, but you get to see the world," he teased. Then he studied her face. "Does absence make your heart grow fonder, or does it just give you the chance to flirt with other men?"

Sheila pulled away from him and let the breeze blow away his comment. "Did you go to the party without me?"

"You know I had to go." He opened the passenger door and motioned for her to get in.

"Did you take someone?"

"I never promise to turn into a hermit when you're away," Spencer said, walking over to his side. "I know you don't."

Sheila's laughter echoed against the adobe wall of the condominium complex. "So if I'm true to you, you'll be true to me?"

"Isn't that the way it's supposed to work?" he questioned.

Marissa waited until they had driven out of sight before emerging from her hiding place. She hurried across the parking lot, where Sheila's laughter still seemed to echo. Spencer was definitely attracted to her. *But what man wouldn't be?* Marissa thought to herself. She had a model's figure and face. Her voice was pitched a little high, but Spencer didn't seem to mind.

What was she doing thinking about Spencer, anyway? As soon as she found Michael, she would be leaving this island and everyone on it behind. Suddenly the Bible verse she held in her hand not only applied to God having plans about Michael's welfare, but about her future as well. She would have a life after this—hopefully meet a man who shared her faith and could understand what she'd been through. That would be later, though—for now, she needed to stay focused on finding Michael.

Sixteen

Marissa knew the reason John hadn't been breathing down her lightly tanned neck for the past week was because he had seen her with Spencer at the King Kamehameha party.

"Look, John, I'm not dating Spencer, so you don't have to be nice to me," she finally told him, tired of his subservient behavior.

John seemed offended. "Have you ever considered that I do some things without a what's-in-it-for-me attitude?"

"No."

John looked at her with a shake of the head. "Be judgmental."

"There's a big difference between being judgmental and being honest."

"You're a church-goer, aren't you?"

"I'm a Christian, if that's what you're asking."

"I thought you were." He lifted his chin slightly. "You probably think I'm going straight to hell because I cheated on my wife."

"I think it's best to leave the judging up to God."

"But you think what I'm doing is sinful, right?"

"By 'doing' do you mean leaving your wife and lying to girlfriends, or would it also include using hotel rooms without paying?"

"How would you know about the rooms?"

"Just a guess." Marissa glanced down at her watch. "I better get going. I'm leaving early tonight, remember? Or don't I qualify for favors anymore?"

"I'm a true gentleman when it comes to agreements—and other things," John said, his trademark sneer returning.

ॐ   ॐ   ॐ   ॐ

The building that housed the seminar was farther away than Marissa realized, and she admonished herself for not starting out earlier. Finally she arrived at the two-story building, which looked exactly like the hand-drawn picture on the map they'd provided—offices in front and a warehouse in the rear. Marissa walked in through the glass entryway, glanced at her watch, and frowned. She was ten minutes late.

A few people looked up as she opened the door to the office suite and quickly found one of the only vacant chairs near the back. A professionally dressed woman in her mid-thirties was speaking. Scanning the room, Marissa's heart pounded hard when she saw Steve Porter sitting off to the left near the podium. She was glad for the twenty-five or so people between them.

Masking her aversion with a pleasant expression, she listened to the woman's presentation on inner feelings, validation, and support. Marissa said a silent prayer thanking God for the gift of discernment and the Holy Spirit.

When the woman spoke of being able to offer individual life-affirming direction, Marissa felt slightly chilled—both physically and mentally. What exactly was the "power" in the "Power for Success" course?

An hour later Steve announced a ten-minute break, and soon the room was rife with conversation. Marissa felt relieved for the recess, not realizing how tense she had become. A middle-aged woman with deep-set eyes and shoulder-length red hair stood behind Marissa in the line that had quickly formed for coffee. Renae Howard was written in block letters on her name tag.

"Did I miss much in the first few minutes of class?" Marissa asked, catching her eye.

Renae shook her head. "Just introductions and a few rules, like not copying the material because of copyright laws. Oh, and to always wear your name tag," she added with a smile.

"Oops," Marissa said, putting her hand where her name tag should have been. "That must be in the packet I haven't opened yet. I'm Marissa Tomsen." They shook hands and Marissa filled her coffee cup and stepped aside for Renae. "I didn't know how far this place was from Kaanapali. I'll have to start out a whole lot earlier next time."

"You live in Kaanapali?" Renae asked.

Marissa nodded. "Near the Regency in the Laloni Complex."

"I'm only two blocks down from you. We're one of those stubborn families who won't sell our beach front property. The lot is worth a fortune but I couldn't bear selling. I've lived there for twenty-two years."

"I wouldn't be able to sell it, either," Marissa said, thinking about her parents' estate. "Home is home no matter how much money it's worth."

Renae looked surprised. "I can't remember the last person who took my side on my decision not to sell. Most people say I'm crazy not to take the money and run. My ex is convinced that's what I'm going to do. He thinks my getting the house was unfair even though he's the one who walked out. I know now he regrets chasing after that girl when he could have had a million dollars." She laughed, and yet there was sadness in her eyes, as if she still loved him.

"Do you have children?" Marissa asked.

"Three. My daughter's married and lives on the mainland, and my son's divorced and back home for now. And then there's the baby, Jeff. He's twelve." Renae took a sip of coffee. "Where do you work?"

"The Regency," Marissa said and then paused, remembering that all attendees were to have managerial positions. She found herself claiming her position with Jonah Stevens. "I'm in public relations."

"I know someone who works in your PR department," Renae said as a nervousness began building in Marissa's chest. "No," she added, rethinking. "Come to think of it, he works for the Hyatt."

Relieved, Marissa moved the conversation back to Renae. "So what do you do?"

"I'm an accountant. One of those big firms with lots of names," she said with a wave of her hand. "I'm a real workaholic. I think my boss sent me here for the reducing stress part."

"Your company sent you here—paid for you?"

"Of course." She gave Marissa an impish grin. "I'm supposed to end up less stressed, less judgmental, more productive, and self-improved. What boss would turn that down?"

If a Christian organization offered the same results, most bosses would, thought Marissa, the whole concept bothering her. But she kept her opinion to herself. "Since we live close," Marissa said, "maybe we could carpool."

"Sure, why not," Renae said. "What's your condo number and I'll—" They were cut off by Steve's tapping on the microphone, signaling that the break was over. "We better arrange this later," Renae whispered. Marissa nodded and they returned to their seats.

❧   ❧   ❧   ❧

As the others walked out to their cars after class, Marissa and Renae stood in the building foyer and exchanged addresses and phone numbers. "And don't worry about taking turns. I can drive every night," Renae said, shaking her head as Marissa attempted to protest. "Then I won't have to worry if it's my night or yours. I'm terribly forgetful."

"Okay, but I'm paying for gas."

"No, that's—" Renae suddenly yanked up her sleeve and checked her watch, looking as if she'd left something on her burner at home. "Oh no. I promised to pick Jeff up from his friend's house half an hour ago." She took the last few steps toward the door and pulled it open. "Sorry for running off, but I better go. I'll pick you up on Wednesday." She threw back a hasty wave as she hurried toward her car.

Marissa waved back, set her purse and books on a nearby couch, and slipped on her blazer. She felt good about their carpool connection and again acknowledged how God was always providing for her. In just the few minutes they had talked, Marissa could see in Renae a person looking for answers and fulfillment. Hopefully their friendship would develop and Marissa would be able to tell her about Jesus and the rock-solid hope only He offers.

Turning back to the couch, Marissa saw that her purse had slipped off and the contents were on the floor. She knelt down and began stuffing things back inside, wishing she'd used her belt bag instead. After retrieving a case of lipstick that had slid halfway under a nearby chair, Marissa stood up. A shiver passed through her as though there had been a sudden change in temperature.

Glancing around the dimly lit foyer and down the even darker hall, she realized she was alone. Or, worse yet, that Steve lurked in the darkness somewhere. Apprehensive about her isolated position, Marissa snatched up the last few items, grabbed her books, and hurried out the door.

She walked quickly toward the car, her espadrilles echoing on the pavement as if in competition with the hammering of her pulse. The unusual shadows cast by the palm trees and the pitch black sky wasn't new to her since she'd become accustomed to leaving the Regency late at night, but something else was—the feeling of a presence hovering near her, stalking her, even though her furtive glances confirmed that no one was there.

With growing uneasiness she peered across the grassy field that bordered the lot and then toward the silhouette of a radio station tower that materialized in the distance. There was no one in sight, and the parking lot was empty except for her car and one other. Still she sensed something . . . someone. Her throat tightened, making it hard for her to swallow.

Instinctively, she ran the last steps to the car, took a quick glance in the back window, hopped in the driver's seat, then fumbled for the automatic door lock button. She jammed the keys in the ignition, and when the engine roared to life she began to scold herself about being paranoid. She hadn't seen or heard anyone.

Then a look in the rearview mirror showed a shadowy figure approaching fast. She rammed the car's shift into drive and floored the gas pedal, all her fears returned. A stop sign blurred as she raced past. Putting all thoughts of safety aside, she took the curves fast and made it back to the highway in record time. Only after she was moving along with other cars did she let up on the accelerator and raise a shaky hand to her forehead. If Steve meant to scare her, he had. Her heart wouldn't stop its frantic beat.

Considering safety in numbers, Marissa drove to the hotel and attempted making it to the break room unnoticed.

"What are you doing here?" Lynn asked, walking over. "I thought you were taking the night off."

"I came by for . . . something in my locker," Marissa said, hoping Lynn wouldn't ask what the something was.

"You seem shook up."

"Oh, some idiot driver nearly ran into me. Have you . . . umm . . . have you seen Spencer? I mean, did he come in for dinner tonight?"

Lynn shook her head. "No, he didn't." She paused. "That's strange. It's Saturday, too." Then she looked toward the kitchen. "Orders up, gotta go. See you tomorrow."

"Yeah, tomorrow," Marissa echoed back.

Marissa stared at the inside of her locker for a few minutes, wondering what had ever possessed her to ask about Spencer. He had protected her before, but it wouldn't be wise to run to him for every scare she had. He had his own life.

She drove home, dead-bolted the door, and pulled the

drapes shut, wondering how much Steve knew about her. The address she had provided on the seminar application had been the hotel's, and she felt sure no one had followed her. It had been childish to run to the restaurant. She was safe here.

Seventeen

*T*he morning light seemed to chase away Marissa's fears of the previous evening. She slipped into a white and navy shirt dress, then headed south down a one-lane road to the church she'd attended her first two Sundays on the island. Myrtle and Ernest had recommended this quaint little church—Prince of Peace—and she wished she could attend every week. But without a car, she'd been limited to the mobile church that met in a Regency ballroom.

Walking in the tiny building, she again admired the simplicity of the rugged wooden cross behind the altar and welcomed the smell and sound of the ocean just outside the open windows. She slid into a half-filled pew, feeling as though she had found a haven from the rest of the world, especially the lies and half-truths she was forced to hear in the "Power for Success" course. The service opening was spoken in Hawaiian—a soft, rolling, melodic language—and the first hymn was one of her father's favorites.

"God always takes care of his own," she remembered her father saying, his voice strong and sure. *"When you two kids were just toddlers, your mother and I taught you to pray. You'll always remember to turn everything over in prayer, won't you Marissa?"*

She had been trying, yet even though her morning prayer time remained consistent, she couldn't feel a precise direction of what God wanted her to do next. Slightly disillusioned, she was eager to hear a powerful, gospel-based sermon.

As the hymn ended, a movement caused Marissa to look toward the doorway. She was startled to see Spencer walk in and slip into a pew near the back. He seemed as surprised as she when their eyes met. Marissa returned her focus to the pastor, but some of her attention was averted to self-consciousness. Part of her resented his being there—as if he was invading her privacy. But part of her felt a lurch of excitement in knowing that he was there. It was a strange mix of feelings.

After the service Marissa took her time putting her hymnal back in its cubby hole, wanting to give Spencer a chance to leave if that's what he preferred. But evidently that wasn't what he wanted at all.

"Marissa!" he said, walking over. "Good to see you . . . especially here." He flashed her a smile that illumined his clear blue eyes.

"Thanks," she said, his enthusiasm diluting her resentment. "Since I had a rental car this weekend, I ventured out. I've been here twice before, though."

Spencer hesitated, then seemed to understand. "You went to the first service, I bet." Marissa nodded. "I usually go to the late one."

Marissa wondered what persuaded him to get up early this morning. "You're a regular here, then?"

"For almost four years. Doesn't seem that long, though."

"He's handy, too," an elderly gentleman interjected as he walked up and paused beside them. "See that railing over there?" He pointed to the front of the church. "He fixed the wobbling thing. And if I'm not too forgetful, he also rebuilt the outside porch."

"You are forgetful, Tim," Spencer said, giving the man a friendly pat on the back. "I only helped a whole team of people with that porch." Spencer turned toward Marissa. "Marissa, this is Tim Lund, head usher."

"What a title." Tim laughed as he shook Marissa's hand. "I'm the only usher."

"How about joining me for brunch?" Spencer asked after they walked out the door and into the bright sunshine. "I know of a great little cafe right near the beach."

"I'd better not," Marissa said, her mind floundering for a plausible excuse.

"Come on," he urged, sensing her hesitation. "You have to eat. And by the way, how's your ankle?"

"A little tender. Of course, the guy who helped bandage it warned me about that."

"That's right, he did," Spencer said with a wink. He walked over, opened the passenger door of his car, and waited.

Marissa shook her head at his insistence, but his attentive manner secretly thrilled her. Marissa decided to set aside her apprehension and accepted his offer, gracefully climbing into the vehicle. The top was down on the convertible, and Marissa enjoyed the sensation of the wind in her hair and the sun on her face. Still, she couldn't help think about who usually occupied this seat. "Is Sheila out of town again?"

"No," Spencer said. "She just doesn't like getting up early." There was no malice in his voice, yet no apologies, either. Marissa let the subject drop, but after Spencer parked near the cafe, he turned toward her and revisited the topic. "I need to say something," he said slowly, as if choosing his words carefully. "I'm not married. I'm not even engaged. But I am dating Sheila, and if that's not comfortable for you, I understand. I realize you're only going to be in Maui for a short time, and I enjoyed your company at the banquet and seeing you now in church, and I just thought—" He paused, looking down at the steering wheel.

"That we could be friends?" Marissa inquired, touched by his honesty.

"Yeah," he agreed, meeting her eyes with instant camaraderie. "I know it's sort of an odd situation, but—"

"You don't have to explain." Marissa suddenly relaxed. "I certainly haven't for you. And yes, I'd like to be friends. I'd like that a lot." She had missed her friends back home immensely, and Spencer's offer seemed like a gift, especially if they shared similar beliefs.

"How did you find Prince of Peace?" Spencer said after they served themselves at the buffet and were seated at an outside table with an umbrella overhead. "We're kind of out of the way, so we don't get many tourists."

"Some friends of mine told me about it. The Thibedeauxes. Myrtle and—"

"Ernest," Spencer finished. Marissa looked surprised, and Spencer chuckled at the irony. "Ernest was one of the guys who helped us repair the church porch. They're real active in the church when they spend their two months on the island every year."

"They go to my church at home the rest of the year," Marissa said, feeling a sudden sense of security with Spencer. "They've been like parents to me ever since mine died." Marissa paused, then answered the obvious question in his eyes. "It was an auto accident. Nine months ago."

"I'm sorry," Spencer murmured softly, sounding like he really felt for her. "I know how much it can hurt. It was rough for me when my dad died. I can't imagine losing both parents at the same time."

Marissa looked out toward the ocean for a moment, considering a bittersweet memory. "We used to come to Maui as a family. Mom and I loved the heat, and Dad and Michael couldn't get enough of the ocean. They snorkeled all the time."

"Do you snorkel?"

Marissa shook her head violently. "Water sports and I aren't compatible. Just putting my face in a pool makes me feel like I'm drowning. I can't even float."

"It would be a good idea to learn. Especially since you're living on an island."

"Believe me, I've tried."

"In the ocean? Salt water helps you float."

"So I'm told," Marissa said, reaching for her iced tea. "Believe me, I'm just not cut out for water sports."

"I know this sounds presumptuous," Spencer said in the car on the way back, "but how about a helicopter ride Tuesday? I have to make a delivery to Hana. That way you can see the east end of the island without having to drive that obnoxiously narrow highway. I know it's your day off," he added with a smile.

"I see that being the boss has advantages." Marissa tried to sound miffed.

"Seven o'clock Tuesday morning, then," Spencer said, pulling up beside her car in the church parking lot.

"I haven't said yes," Marissa complained, getting out of his car.

"You didn't agree to lunch, either," Spencer observed with a smile. "See you bright and early."

Eighteen

*I*t was the middle of the night, but Michael was keenly alert. Pulling the hanger out from its hiding place under the mattress, he walked silently to the door. Listening first to make sure a guard wasn't making the rounds, he inserted the now-straightened wire into the lock. With sticky, sweaty hands, he pushed hard against the mechanism in the back and then worked the wire up and down and back and forth. He labored until his hands grew sore with the continuous pushing and pulling. Nothing he tried released the lock.

Pausing, he looked behind him again at the small window near the ceiling, wishing for the umpteenth time it was bigger. There was no way he could fit through the opening. Besides, most evenings the guards had a campfire on the beach just a few feet away. They were close enough for Michael to hear their voices but too far away to make out what they were saying. It didn't matter anyway.

Frustrated, he turned back to his task, carefully working the lock again. If he made it out, would he run to Lauren or Marissa first? Why had Lauren left him, anyway? Hadn't he been romantic enough? She was so great to be with. A little consumed with her career, maybe, but she had a right to be. She was an excellent reporter. And she just had a way about her that he admired. He must not have been all that to her. Michael sighed and shook his head. Maybe he didn't mean anything at all.

An instant later the door burst open and two guards ran in. Caught in the act of trying to escape, Michael was thrown to the floor, and the hanger slashed repeatedly across his back. With every strike his hate for the guards and his situation intensified. Minutes later, alone and lying on bloodstained sheets, Michael vowed to get even—vowed to kill them all. He imagined himself after the massacre being led away in handcuffs. Yes, he had done it. Yes, it was self-defense. No, no one believed him. No, Lauren wouldn't visit him in prison. The thoughts were absurd, but he continued thinking them anyway, and for the first time he had the horrible thought that he would never escape, that he would die there.

Michael rolled over and then winced when the dried blood peeled away from the mattress, exposing raw skin. What evil motivated these men to do this? What more did they want from him? Constant headaches were prevalent now. He attributed them to the "vitamins" they gave him each day. The tapes had become a part of his life. Sometimes he felt capable of tuning them out. Other times he felt completely helpless to their sway and found himself repeating along with the words, then later feeling terrified when some of the thoughts seemed to become his own. After being confined there for two weeks, he could only conclude that they never planned to release him. He had to find a way out. He had to.

৯৫   ৯৫   ৯৫   ৯৫

Five days later, Michael's back had scabbed over, but hatred had infected his soul. He drank his "vitamin" in the cafeteria hoping it to be his last. He had developed a plan—a carefully thought out way of escape. He sat at the far table watching the dark-shirted crew members unload the supply boat. If today was the same as any weekday, they would make several trips hauling supplies to the back door and then disappear inside for three to five minutes. He hoped that would be enough time. It had to be. The hanger beating had resolved within him the decision to try to escape.

Michael ate without tasting, his mouth mechanically chewing and swallowing without recognition of the action. His stomach churned nervously, and the smell of broccoli made him slightly nauseous. He forced down the natural fare anyway, not wanting to do anything different today than any other. After his last bite, he walked to the huge dumpster and aimed his plate off to the right. The ocean breeze caught the plate exactly as he'd hoped. Acting disgusted for the benefit of the others who were milling about, he walked to the side of the dumpster and pretended to retrieve the plate. Seeing no one in sight, he took a step beyond and slipped behind the huge metal container, out of everyone's view.

His heart beat violently. Had anyone noticed? Could he pull this off? He crouched down and forced himself to wait a full minute. After all remained calm, he eased himself away from the dumpster, crawled fifteen feet to a shrub, and hid behind its large leaves. From the inside waist of his pants, he pulled out the dark T-shirt he'd been wearing the day he arrived at the camp and yanked it on over his head. He hoped in some strange way that his putting it back on meant he was going to succeed in getting out. Underneath his white baggy pants he wore cutoffs. He had spent hours carefully making a trail of thin holes at thigh length in his jeans, then ripped them off. He hoped now he looked like one of the crew.

Peering out toward the dock, he anxiously eyed the supply boat that was more than a hundred feet away. The "vitamins" made it difficult to stay centered on one thought for long, and he found himself panicking. Forcing several deep breaths, he waited until the last box was hauled to the kitchen entrance. The men disappeared inside. He had to move—now.

Michael stood, his heart hammering like a pahu drum. His knees nearly buckled on his first few steps, but he quickly caught himself and emerged from the bushes, pretending to be zipping his fly. He forced even, quick steps. One of the resort guards looked over at him, but Michael acted inattentive, and he breathed a ragged sigh of relief when the man made no attempt to stop him.

Walking out on the unmanned dock, Michael bent down near the front rope that secured the boat, pretending to tie his shoe. He loosened the knot and slipped the line into the water. A tremendous rush of adrenaline filled his being when he stepped on board and crouched down low to untie the back. Could it be that in just a few moments he would be free?

Crawling on the fiberglass floor, he slid the cabin door open, and in one quick movement, he was at the wheel. To his delight, the keys were in the ignition. The big moment he'd dreamed about for weeks was becoming reality. He planned to gun the engine and head full speed, straight ahead. Only after he was out of shooting range would he sit in the chair and take a course.

With trembling hands, he turned the key. Just as the engine rumbled to life, a well-muscled canine body rushed at him from the cabin below. Letting go of the throttle and jerking backward, Michael witnessed the Rottweiler's teeth snap savagely together. He grabbed a wooden fish knocker and flailed wildly, but he was no match for the trained attack dog. Nauseous pain rippled up his leg when the dog lunged again, this time sinking his incisors deep into Micheal's calf.

Excited voices and pounding footsteps on the dock made Michael reach once more for the throttle—for the freedom he could almost taste. But the butt of a gun slammed against his head and he dropped to the cabin floor.

Nineteen

"You made it," Spencer called up to Marissa as she walked down the outside staircase to the parking lot. Spencer, wearing a tank top and shorts, was loading gear into the trunk of his car. "Hope you have a swimsuit and sunscreen along. You can't visit Hana and not spend a few minutes on the beach."

"Got it. Brought my camera, too." Marissa motioned to her bulging tote bag. "Thought I'd play tourist."

"Great. I'll practice my flight-seeing monologue on you then."

"Is that a promise or a threat?" Marissa asked, her eyes dancing mischievously.

"We're pretty spunky first thing in the morning, aren't we?"

"Amazing, huh, since I even had to work late last night."

"You aren't one for sleeping in, though," Spencer noted, closing the trunk.

Marissa narrowed her eyes to study his face. "How would you know how late I sleep?"

"You live right above me. I can hear water running, the floor creaking—stuff like that."

Marissa looked at him in feigned indignation and said, "If I could move to another unit, I would."

"Would you?" Spencer asked, letting his eyes wander over her face. Marissa wanted to flirt back, but common sense urged her to abandon the idea, and she simply handed him her bag and climbed in the front seat.

"Well, there she is," Spencer said after a bumpy road led them to an unpaved runway. He led her over to a sleek-bodied red helicopter, immaculately clean with black call letters on the side.

"It's wonderful!" she said, eyes wide with surprise. "I was expecting something smaller and much . . . I don't know . . . I mean, aren't these things expensive? How can you afford just to haul bottled water?"

"Don't forget the sunscreen," he said with a chuckle. "The tourists really go for that."

Marissa raised her eyebrows, waiting.

"Actually, I got a really good deal on her. A flight-seeing business was going belly-up and she was nearing her TBO—total hours before overhaul. Theo, an aircraft mechanic friend, helped me with some of the money and all the repairs. Still, it wasn't cheap. I owe the bank a whole lot."

"Another reason to keep your job at the Regency?"

"Exactly," Spencer said as he began removing the exhaust and blade covers. She watched him curiously. "We put these on to protect against blowing sand and birds who think chopper exhausts are great places to build nests."

"Serious?"

"Serious," he said. "Choppers don't mix well with birds, on the ground or in the air."

"I think I get the picture," Marissa said, scrunching up her eyebrows as they walked back to the car for the gear.

Spencer finished checking the helicopter body, then opened the left door, saying, "All aboard."

"This is going to be great," Marissa pronounced, walking to the right side and pulling on the door handle.

"You can sit on that side if you want to," Spencer called over to her, "but then you'd have to fly it, too."

Realizing her error, she joined him on the copilot side. "I'm really showing my ignorance," she said, rolling her eyes.

"Don't worry." Spencer gave her a wink. "You're not the first to want to get in on that side. Here's your seat belt." He handed her one end of the harness. "Put your arms through here and here and then clasp it like this."

Her stomach fluttered when their hands touched, and she caught herself wondering what it would be like to hold his hand and know his attention in a romantic way. But she quickly dismissed the thoughts, realizing how futile they were.

"Weather's perfect today," Spencer said, getting in on the other side. "Hana's just a short hop, but we'll take the long way and get in a little more flight-seeing." Spencer put on his seat belt and performed the pre-flight check while Marissa studied the instrument panel, intrigued.

"I haven't been in anything this small since my uncle Hiram took me flying in his two-seater plane when I was a kid. On my first and last ride with him, he did a few stalls and some other horsing around. I told him I took my life more seriously than that."

"Don't worry. I do, too. My dad was a tough instructor. He flew these in the Air Force. Taught me plenty of tight maneuvers and had me perform enough full autos to the ground for a lifetime of flying."

"What's a full auto to the ground?" Marissa questioned, looking over at him.

"That's when you land your chopper without an engine." He gave her a smile. "If I can help it, we won't do one today."

Spencer flipped a few switches, and the engine and then the rotors came to life, causing a flock of sparrows to lift and scatter en masse. He retrieved two headsets and handed her one. "Put this on." His voice rose above the rotor's noise. "You'll be able to hear the radio and, of course, my gripping commentary."

Marissa slipped the band on her head and fidgeted with the mouthpiece that felt awkwardly close to her mouth. "Can you hear me?" she shouted.

Spencer's hands flew up to his ears and he grimaced. "Gone are the days when you had to yell at each other," Spencer said, talking in a normal voice through the headset, "although that has its place, too." Marissa apologized in a softer voice, thankful for his good nature.

A moment later the chopper lifted off the ground and hovered while Spencer had a short conversation with the tower. Then, as if released from a rope, the chopper rose and swayed forward. Marissa looked out the bubble window, awed by the lifting sensation and thrilled over seeing the island from this angle.

"See the church?" Spencer said, pointing off to his left. Small as it was, the white steeple stood out poignantly on the grassy knoll bordering the ocean. Sugarcane fields and variegated sandy beaches offered a unique view, and then came postcard vistas of deep bays and luxuriant green valleys. Marissa's heart raced when Spencer hovered dramatically close to waterfalls plunging hundreds of feet down the mountain spines. This was a Maui she'd never seen before.

"I feel as if I own that waterfall and that beach," Marissa said, laughing.

"There's no one within miles to contest your claim," Spencer replied with a broad smile, hovering a moment longer before continuing. "See over there?" Spencer motioned toward a cliffside road that wound dangerously close to the rugged coastline and then disappeared back into the deep, lush jungle. "That's the road to Hana."

"Are you playing tour guide?" Marissa looked expectantly at Spencer, liking the strong angles of his face and the way his lips moved over his straight white teeth.

Spencer cleared his throat and began talking in an obviously deeper voice. "Along the fifty-three mile drive to Hana, there are six hundred seventeen turns and fifty-six miniature bridges."

"Ooh, a number guy. I'm impressed," Marissa teased in a playful, sultry voice. Suddenly the chopper tipped forward and hovered in place. Marissa's hands flew to her stomach.

"Next time you interrupt, you'll be ejected from your seat," Spencer commanded, his voice filled with mock intimidation.

Marissa saluted. "Aye, aye pilot."

"Now, where was I?" Spencer said, piloting forward again. "Oh yes." He cleared his throat again. "Before they paved the road to Hana using convict labor, the road was constantly washing out. It was common to see drivers swap cars at impassable sections, continue on in one another's cars, and then meet back and trade for the return trip. Even today some people who have white-knuckled it will swear by a blood oath never to drive it again." He pulled the helicopter up and away from the highway. "Now over there is the island of—" Spencer put out his hand and covered her eyes. "You did pay for the ultra-deluxe tour, didn't you?"

"Of course," Marissa said, giggling.

"Okay, then." He removed his hand. "The island you see in the distance is the big island, Hawaii. To our east is the smallest island, Kahoolawe. The Polynesian demigod, Maui, is credited for having fished all the Hawaiian islands up from the sea, although geologists have their own version of the events. They say that the islands were formed by massive volcanoes."

"You're a natural at this," Marissa said, admiration in her eyes. "The bank president needs to take a trip with you."

"You betcha," Spencer said with a lopsided grin that caused her pulse to quicken.

She dropped her gaze to the fields stylized into neat agrarian checkerboards, trying to focus on the tour and not the guide. "What are they growing?" she said.

"Taro and watercress. Have you ever eaten poi?"

Marissa shook her head.

"They make poi from taro roots. It's nutritious, but pretty bland. Of course, everyone has to try it once."

After passing miles of fields, the terrain became jungle again. Spencer pointed ahead, smiling. "I used to make deliveries there."

"On the beach?" Marissa asked, not seeing anything else.

"No. There's a building down there. But the people who own the property don't allow motorized vehicles or choppers on their grounds, so I air drop. You know, open the door and drop it out."

"You're kidding, right?"

"No," Spencer said, shaking his head. "It's the truth. I didn't do very well on my first drop," Spencer added, chuckling. "The duffel bag hit the tree and tore open. All this white material, bedding I guess, was strewn in the trees, billowing in the wind."

"What did the people on the ground do?"

"They cussed me out on the radio and then climbed the trees and got the stuff, I guess."

"And you never heard from them again, right?" Marissa smiled as Spencer headed the helicopter inland again.

"Actually, I made quite a few deliveries for them. None as elegant as the first, though."

The road serpentined under them several more times before Spencer dropped below tree level and then flashed her a grin. "Okay, the tour's over. This is us setting down." The pads gently touched the ground in the middle of a field, and Spencer pushed several buttons as the rotors whirred to a stop.

A dark-complected young man with crooked, yellowing teeth approached the chopper, nodded hello, and silently unloaded the supplies into a waiting jeep. After securing the helicopter covers, Spencer motioned Marissa over to the vehicle. "Take the passenger seat," he said. "The store's just down the road."

"Where are you going to ride?" Marissa said, looking behind her at the tightly packed jeep.

"Guess I'll just have to hang on, huh, Joey?" Spencer said with a grin to the young man.

"Don't know—can you?" Joey countered, a challenge in his voice as the jeep lurched forward. Spencer ran alongside, caught up, then grabbed the rollbar and balanced on the side step. The two men laughed as they bumped along the dirt road, red dust billowing and country music blaring.

Minutes later they arrived at the store that stocked everything from diapers to diving masks. Spencer introduced Marissa to the owner, Leon, who looked like an older version of the driver.

"Thanks, Spencer," Leon said, pulling a pen from his shirt pocket. "You saved me. A whole busload of tourists bought lots of *da kine*." He motioned toward a rack of tourist paraphernalia, grinning. "Have to have that stuff or they might not come back, eh?" He initialed the receipt.

Spencer laughed. "Say, I was wondering if I could use the jeep for a few hours."

Leon looked over at Marissa and smiled. "No problem. Enjoy some time with the pretty *wahine*."

Spencer thanked him and a moment later they were in the jeep again—this time the music subdued. "Now for the sites," Spencer said. "Here's Hana."

"Where?"

"We just passed it."

Marissa rolled her eyes. "I get it. What's next?"

"Seven sacred pools. That is, if we can fight the tour buses."

They arrived at the pools, but the area was crawling with people—and ants. "They love brunettes," Spencer said, watching Marissa flick two tiny black ants off her leg with a look of disdain.

"Let's go," Spencer said. "I know of a perfect beach. Great for swimming—you'll be out in the water in minutes."

"*You* can go in the water," Marissa said, continuing to brush off real and imaginary ants as they walked back. "I'll stay on the beach."

Twenty

*B*etter put on your tennis shoes," Spencer suggested when he parked the jeep at the end of a dirt road. "It's a short hike, but it's steep and the rocks tend to avalanche in places."

"Avalanche?" Marissa said as she slipped off her sandals and reached for her shoes. "I don't remember ants *or* avalanches the last time I was in Maui."

"You didn't see much, then," Spencer said as he grabbed his day pack and swung the jeep door shut. Marissa smiled to herself, liking his confidence.

The trail began with a gentle downward slope and then turned treacherously steep. Sharp, red volcanic cinders soon ran like water around and past their feet.

"Think of it as dry-land surfing," Spencer said with a good-natured grin as he ran a few steps and then held out his arms, sliding with the fast-moving cinders.

Marissa followed, swaying erratically and trying not to fall backward or pitch forward. Using her skiing skills, she managed to avoid the palm trees and then use the last two to slow down and then stop. She arrived at the bottom dusty but upright.

"That was different," she said, still holding onto the last palm tree with an uncertain smile. The red dust on her shoes and calves were evidence of her adventure. She began to brush it off but paused and straightened back up when she noticed the view.

They had entered paradise.

Before them sat a sparkling red rock beach with a natural lava pinnacle barrier forming a protected in-shore pool. The dazzling blue ocean gently caressed the shore, and a warm breeze ruffled the bordering fronds and palm trees.

"This is beautiful," Marissa whispered.

"Great, isn't it?" Spencer said. "Whenever I come here I feel as though I've discovered a place no one else has. Maybe it's the cliffs all around or—"

"No tourists," Marissa finished for him, smiling.

"Touché. They're our bread and butter, but sometimes . . ."

They walked around the beach exploring—theirs the only footprints. "I'm going to enjoy this respite and not worry about how we're going to hike back up," Marissa said as she picked a spot halfway to the water and spread out her beach towel.

"There is an easier path . . . it's just not as scenic." Spencer smiled broadly as he took his snorkeling fins and mask out of his backpack.

"Of course," Marissa said with a sigh. "With you I should have known."

"I'll leave you alone to tan as promised," Spencer said, pulling off his tank top. "But after you're baked, you're getting a swimming lesson."

"No thanks," Marissa replied, applying a dose of sunscreen. "But nice try." He could enjoy the ocean, she thought, settling back on her towel to drink in the sun's rays. For her, the beach was enough.

Twenty minutes later, Marissa stood. The breeze had become almost non-existent and she was sweltering from the midday sun. Spencer was snorkeling near the lava barrier that buffered the waves, and the crystal blue water looked appealing. She walked to the water's edge and at first just let the water lap gently against her feet. Then she noticed some brightly colored fish and waded in up to her waist.

A few minutes later she heard Spencer whistle and saw him grinning over at her. "This is as far as I go," she yelled. "And I don't need any laughing from the peanut gallery."

"I wouldn't laugh," he said, paddling over and tossing his snorkeling gear on the beach. "Not knowing how to swim is serious business." And to Marissa's surprise he looked serious. "Can you keep yourself afloat? Anything?"

"Only this," Marissa said, taking a few more steps and then showing him a laborious dog paddle.

"Try it this way," he said, cupping his hands. She tried again, improving considerably, but still obviously afraid of going in over her head.

"That's better. Now, can you float on your back?"

"No. I've never been able to do that," she said, fear showing in her eyes.

"The key is to relax."

"I know, but I just can't."

"You can," Spencer countered.

"No," Marissa said, turning back toward the beach. "Others have tried. I'm just not meant to swim."

"I'm not like the others. I know I can teach you."

Marissa paused and considered him. "What makes you so sure?"

"I just know. Besides, where could you get a more perfect place to learn?" He gestured around the cove as if it were his backyard.

Or a more handsome instructor, she thought.

He put out his hand. "I promise I won't let you sink."

Surprising even herself, she gave in. Spencer helped her lie back in the water as he supported her. Her body was stiff and she considered the exercise another wasted effort. "Relax," he said. "Take a deep breath and then blow it out. Look up at the clouds. Pretend you're floating up there with them."

"You're going to be holding me up for a long time, and as soon as you let go, I'll sink," she muttered, not liking the feeling of water in her ears.

"I have all day," he answered.

After a while Marissa became acclimated to the water and let her body relax.

"You did it," he said softly. "You're floating."

"Not really. You're holding me up," Marissa said. "It isn't the same."

"No, I'm not. You've been floating on your own for at least a minute." With the knowledge she wasn't being held, Marissa tensed and began to sink. But before her face went underwater, Spencer caught her and set her upright in one smooth motion.

"I was floating?" she asked, smoothing her wet hair back, disbelief in her eyes. "On my own?"

Spencer nodded. "Try it again and you'll see. Next thing you know, you'll be swimming." This time she didn't look at him quite so skeptically.

With Spencer's help she tried again, and before she returned to her beach blanket, she had enough confidence to float completely on her own and add a primitive arm movement. She even attempted holding her breath underwater when she saw some long-nosed butterfly fish swim by. She felt triumphant—as though she had conquered something momentous.

Lying on their towels on the sand, Marissa looked over at Spencer, who was on his back with his eyes shut, taking in the tropical rays. "What made you think you could teach me to swim?"

"Oh, so you're a swimmer now?" he teased, not bothering to open his eyes.

"You know what I mean. How did you know I could do it?"

"I didn't," he said, a slow smile coming to his lips. "But confidence begets confidence, wouldn't you say?"

Twenty-one

After the trek back up the steep incline, Marissa insisted on buying their lunch. They found some hoagies, cheese, crackers, and bottled guava juice in a nearby store and then drove to a scenic pull-off with the ocean below them on one side and a grassy countryside on the other. As they ate, a few cows wandered by.

"It's so different here," Marissa said as the warm breeze dried her hair. "It doesn't feel like the rest of the island."

"It would be great to live on this side. But I've had no experience raising cattle, and I don't think I'd make a very good taro farmer." Spencer's smile lit up his eyes.

"Do you like living here—in Maui, I mean?"

"For the most part. I miss having definite seasons, though. Summer moves into fall and then into winter without much difference. That's why I take winter vacations in Colorado or Alaska. For two weeks, I ski and build snowmen."

Marissa laughed.

"There's time to show you one more place," Spencer said, glancing at his watch and then downing the last of his juice. He grabbed the remains of their lunch and directed Marissa back to the jeep. Initially returning to the highway, Spencer soon took a dirt side road. Large spade-shaped leaves brushed the sides of the jeep, and the jungle became dense with mango, guava, and breadfruit trees that filtered the sunlight overhead.

Spencer parked the jeep and motioned Marissa down a rugged path. "You certainly like the dangerous locales," she said, surveying the steep, rocky path.

"You have to work a little to get to the most beautiful places. Most people are lazy."

"I don't know if I'd call it lazy," Marissa remarked after a mynah bird screeched his disapproval from overhead.

They approached a plateau and Marissa cautiously walked to the edge, eyeing the sheer drop-off and natural pool below. The water was clear and looked only a few feet deep.

"Think I'll try a dive," Spencer said, pulling off his T-shirt. Before Marissa could voice her objection, he disappeared over the side. As if in slow motion, Marissa watched him fall, horrified. His body sliced the water clean, hardly leaving a ripple.

"Spencer!" she screamed as fear flooded through her. He'd been crazy to jump. He'd hit the bottom—break his neck. Couldn't he see that the water wasn't deep enough? Marissa gazed down in horror, her hand clasped over her mouth. How soon would it be before she would see his body float up, limp and broken?

Suddenly Spencer's head reappeared from the water. "Yeeaaah!" he yelled, holding a fist up to her as if in victory. "That got my heart pumping."

Seeing that he was all right, Marissa's anger took precedence over her fear. "Mine too!" she yelled down to him, hands on her hips. "I can't believe you'd try such a stupid stunt. You scared me half to death."

"Then I did it," Spencer said, his laughter ricocheting off the rock walls.

"Did what? Temporarily lose your mind?" she retorted, her voice edged with sarcasm.

"No. Carried on the tradition," he called back up to her. "One of my friends did the same thing to me. Scared the life out of me. I've been waiting to try it on someone else."

"Thanks a load for making me the 'someone else.' "

"You have to admit it's a great dive." Spencer grinned up at her as he treaded water. "The water looks a lot shallower than it is. Want to try?"

"No thanks."

"At least climb down, then. My guess is you've never dog paddled in a cave before."

"Now that was a wild guess," Marissa called to him, but instead of playing poor sport, she tossed her cover-up next to Spencer's discarded T-shirt and made her way down the rocky front. She paused halfway down to look up at the surrounding cliff. A row of dead trees and thick foliage leered out and spilled over the sheer rock wall that plunged to the pool and beyond. She wondered how many people knew of this place.

When she reached the last jut of rock before the water, Spencer swam over and reached up to help her in.

"I don't know," she said, her old fears resurrecting as she gazed into what now appeared to be a bottomless pool.

"Come on in. You have to try this. I'll be right by your side." When Spencer reached for her arm, she wanted to say no but couldn't. He had been wonderful about teaching her to float, and she didn't want to disappoint him now. Turning around, she slipped in the water, inhaling sharply over the initial cold sensation. She held tightly to Spencer as he led her across the pool, and then she attached herself like a barnacle to the rocky side. The igneous rock that jutted out above them became a ceiling, blocking the sun and making the water temperature drop even further.

"Feel the pull of the ocean?" Spencer asked. "It's just on the other side of the wall. The water in here rises and falls with the tide. That's the only thing you have to check on before you dive. If the rocks over there are covered, you're safe. If not, you're taking a chance of hitting the bottom."

"Wonderful," Marissa muttered, cringing at the idea of diving into anything, much less a pool of questionable depth.

"I didn't mean to scare you. Just thought I'd tell you in case you come back here next week and try it yourself." Spencer gave her a mischievous wink as he held out his arm. "Now let's see the cave."

"I thought this was the cave."

"No. It's in through there." He pointed toward the back wall. "I know exactly where the opening is, so you won't have to hold your breath long."

"Hold my breath?" Marissa tightened her barnacle grip.

"Yeah. We swim a couple feet down, then through an opening and voilà, we're there."

"Voilà, you're there," Marissa said. "I'm *not* about to swim underwater."

"Come on. Aren't you curious?"

"Spencer, I've gone from complete fear of the water, to learning to float, to climbing into a pool where I can't even touch the bottom. I think that's progress enough for one day."

"You've accomplished a lot, I know. But you'll really miss out if you don't see this. I'll pull you through so fast, you won't have to hold your breath for more than ten seconds."

Marissa looked across the pool and sighed. "I can't believe I'm even contemplating this."

"Deep down, I know you love a challenge." Their eyes met and held.

"This is going to be a very long ten seconds," she finally said.

"That's more like it." He guided her a few feet over to where a large rock jutted out at shoulder height. "Now, take a few deep breaths and on the count of three, we'll go under."

One . . . two . . . On her third ragged breath, they went under. Down first and then straight ahead, Spencer guided her through a door's-width opening. A few feet past the opening, Spencer pulled her up to the surface. Gasping, she clung to him.

"Are you okay?" he asked, concern showing in his face.

Marissa loosened the stranglehold she had on his arm, realizing that holding her breath hadn't been all that bad, and it had only been ten seconds—she'd counted. "I'm fine. It was just a little different, that's all."

"You can get out of the water if you want." Spencer motioned toward a nearby natural rock ledge. "That is if you don't get too cold."

Marissa pulled herself up on the ledge and then looked around the dimly lit room. The ceiling, damp and moss laden, curved an impressive twenty feet over their heads, filtering sunlight through a papaya-sized hole. "This is unbelievable," Marissa said, then smiled upon hearing the echo of her words. "How did you find this place?"

"Theo, my mechanic friend, took me here a couple years ago. He's a native of the island. Knows lots of places like this."

Spencer joined her on the ledge, their bare arms and legs touching because of the cramped space. Marissa felt the same unwelcome surge of excitement as when Spencer had appeared at her door in a tux. She didn't dare look at him for fear he could feel the dizzying current racing through her.

"You'll have to meet Theo. He's a great guy. His family is fun, too. He has nine siblings. Whenever they get together it feels like a party."

There was a short silence and Spencer looked her way. Their eyes held for a moment, and Marissa was suddenly acutely aware of his body next to hers. She looked up at the ceiling, her heart pounding.

Spencer's gaze followed Marissa's. "The ceiling is great, isn't it?"

"Yes, it's strange with it being so high and with walls all around. It's so . . . so private."

"I'm realizing that," Spencer said softly, not allowing the cave to repeat his words.

When their gaze met again, she felt her skin warm and her heart pound even more wildly in her chest. It was too easy to get lost in the way he looked at her. Spencer tilted his head as his mouth descended to hers. Wonderful, vibrant feelings of passion coursed through her, different than she'd had for any other man. His strong body felt sure and right, but then she pulled away.

"I don't think this is a good idea," Marissa whispered, looking away, suddenly not knowing what to do with her hands.

"I'm sorry," Spencer said, dropping his arm from around her shoulder. "I didn't mean to bring you here and then—" He studied her face for a moment and then slipped back into the water. "It's cold in here. We better go."

Twenty-two

John appeared sullen when Marissa walked into his office the following Friday to pick up her timecard. Usually he was eager to talk or throw a crude comment her way, but today his manner was somber. His many stacks of paper work had been pushed aside and a computer was squeezed between. Marissa recognized the Macintosh Quadra 650 immediately.

"You don't have to stare," John said glumly, his eyes not leaving the machine.

Like a surfer drawn to the challenge of a wave, Marissa walked behind John and looked at the screen. John mumbled an expletive after he punched a key that only produced an obnoxious beep.

"What program are you using?" Marissa asked.

"Program?" He glanced at his watch and then back to the computer. "Look, I'm behind the eight ball. I don't have time for chitchat."

Marissa eyed the unwrapped manual as he typed in another incorrect key. "Mind if I try?"

"Look, I—" John pulled his eyes from the screen, and then, as if suddenly seeing her in a new light, he stood and offered her his chair. "Sure, go ahead."

Marissa typed in a series of commands, stopped, reworked a formula, and the calculation John had been cursing totaled. "How did you do that?" he asked.

"You weren't that far off," Marissa said, standing. "You just had too many symbols in your formula."

"So you know computers pretty well, huh?"

"Well enough," she said, walking toward the door.

"Wait—" John called, continuing when he had Marissa's attention. "Can you help with a couple other glitches? Management needs these quarterly reports ASAP, and I'm like a fish out of water doing all this stuff."

Marissa looked down at the many pages of handwritten numbers near his elbow. "You've been handwriting your reports?"

"No," he admonished. "I use my brain to get the numbers and then I type them. Old fashioned, but reliable. I'll bet half the college grads can't add as fast as I can."

"You're probably right." Marissa held up her hands, not wanting to fuel a longer discussion.

"So can you help?"

Marissa sighed, thinking how unbearable it would be to work alongside John, even for a short while. Of course, he had juggled the schedules around so she could attend the success seminars—so she felt she owed him something. "All right. I'll come in an hour early tomorrow."

"No. I need you now. The report is due first thing tomorrow morning."

"Who's going to hostess?" she said, frustrated that problems were already surfacing.

"I'll ask Crystal to come in. Or I'll do it myself," John said, obviously anxious to get away from the machine. "There's the packet management sent me," he said, motioning to a manila envelope. "And the notebook next to it has all the numbers that need plugging in. Nothing is top secret, but don't go spouting our profits around. I'll be out here if you have any questions." He grabbed his suit jacket and walked out of the office, noticeably relieved.

Marissa hung her apron on a hook behind the door and slid her purse under the desk, wondering what she was getting into.

Papers were piled nearly everywhere, and yellow sticky notes layered the bulletin board. She moved several stacks of paper work from the desk to a corner on the floor and then sat down. Even though she felt duped into this, something felt good about being behind a computer again. She missed her office, the mahogany desk, neat and shiny, the wonderful view of the river, even her favorite coffee mug. She missed it all. It wasn't fair—her having to be away.

Tears filled her eyes and she bit her lip as she stared at the computer, identical to the one that sat on her desk in Portland. Who was using her office? Had they replaced her? Had Donald? Marissa chastised herself for her petty concerns when her search for Michael still contained so many questions. Struggling to bury the depressing thoughts, she blew cigarette ashes off a stack of papers and then opened the manila envelope. The date on the cover letter was over a month old. John's procrastination was so childlike. Of course, he flew by the seat of his polyester pants in his marriage, so why would he be any different about work?

Marissa plunged into the project, challenged by her own work ethics, and minutes before closing, she took a sip of cold coffee as she rechecked the finished report. John appeared just as the last page was slipping out of the laser printer.

"You're done?" he said, waltzing in the room and glancing at the first few pages, noticeably pleased. "Say, I was thinking . . ." he began.

She smelled liquor on his breath and was indignant over his irresponsibility. "Before or during your drinking session?" Marissa said sharply.

"I wouldn't call one martini a drinking session," John retorted. "Look, I was going to offer you an office job."

"No thanks," Marissa said, picking up her purse and walking to the door.

"I need a person to do stuff like this. I'll increase your hourly by two dollars."

Marissa paused as common sense urged her to accept the offer. But how could she work with him? His irresponsibility this evening only magnified their incompatibility. "No," she said flatly.

"Okay, wait, " John said, sounding desperate. "I'll pay you three more an hour, but that's as high as I can go."

Marissa leaned against the door frame, her back still to him. She sighed in frustration, knowing she couldn't afford to turn down the offer. "I want everything in writing," she said, turning around, "and I still only want to work part-time late afternoon and evening hours." She could picture John agreeing now but reneging after he had sent off the report.

"Sure thing." John grabbed a piece of paper and sat down behind his manual typewriter. He typed with amazing speed, titling the position Administrative Assistant and promising the increased salary to take effect immediately.

"You'll have to agree not to smoke in the office, too," Marissa said, her pen poised above the document.

"I can handle that." John looked relieved after she signed her name. "I'll leave this here, then," he said, pointing to the report. "Could you write a cover letter and deliver it tomorrow?"

"Where will you be?"

"Now, that," he said with a smile as he picked up the phone, "is my business."

Twenty-three

Michael woke with a pounding head and a horrible throbbing in his leg. His right arm was numb because of its awkward position under him, and he groaned when he tried to straighten it. Moonlight cast shadows through a shoulder-high opening secured with thick metal bars. Offensive smells hung heavy in the dankness. Lifting his head a few inches off the cold concrete, he moved to look at his leg and saw a large gash, red and swollen with a pool of blood underneath.

Dizzy and weak, he tried to sit up but failed. He had to stop the bleeding. Had to make a tourniquet. As he fought to try again, a sound brought his attention to the metal door. He watched the handle turn, then a figure appeared, pulling something. Another prisoner? He couldn't see well. When the door closed, the figure approached and Michael covered his face, expecting another beating. Instead, he felt strong arms lift him up onto a mattress.

"Drink this," a man's voice whispered. "It will help you."

With no strength to resist, Michael allowed the man to prop up his head. He struggled to swallow the strong-tasting liquid that immediately warmed his body. After the man lowered Michael back to the mattress, he covered his upper body with a blanket and then moved to inspect Michael's leg. The moonlight revealed the old man's face and Michael stared. This was the sickly lunatic who had sat by him in the truck. He wasn't sick and empty-eyed now. He was strong and alert.

"Who are you?" Michael managed, his tongue feeling thick.

"Try to keep still," the man whispered, pulling items from underneath his tunic as he began cleaning the deep puncture wounds in Michael's leg.

Clenching the mattress, Michael endured the process, perceiving this man meant good. He was woozy and fighting sleep when the old man sutured his leg with quick, practiced movements and then applied some ointment to the bruises on his face. "Sleep now," the man said as he gathered up his supplies. "I'll be back tomorrow."

Michael felt a gentle pat on his arm before he faded completely.

ॐ ॐ ॐ ॐ

The next time Michael woke, he felt a new bandage on his leg, and another day's growth of beard on his face. A shaft of sunlight shone in the upper window and the room was warmer. Turning his head, he felt something near his shoulder. His leg throbbed with pain as he propped himself onto his elbow and discovered a sandwich wrapped in paper toweling. He pushed away the cockroach that had discovered it first, and with trembling hands he ate, savoring the food and appreciating that someone in this hellhole cared about him. He tried to think that God did, but the stark reality of where he was and his condition made him doubt what he once believed. He claimed sleep again.

When darkness returned, so did the old man. He carried in a mop and bucket, then shut the door behind him. Afterward he pulled out a bottle of water and a sandwich from a pocket in his tunic. He gave them to Michael and then dipped the mop into the bucket of water and began scrubbing the blood-stained cement. "I can't come everyday," the man said quietly. "But I'll come as often as I can."

Michael wanted to trust this man, but he had learned that all things come with a cost, and even though this man seemed to be helping him, he was still one of them. He wore the pendant. "What do you people want from me?"

The old man continued mopping and didn't look up. "They want the same things people have been killing on another over for centuries. Power and wealth."

The old man didn't include himself in the group. Michael wondered why.

"Do you pray?" the man suddenly said.

"Pray?" Michael asked, his face hardening into a mask of hatred as he remembered the man's necklace. "To your god or mine?"

The man paused in his work and looked at Michael with clear, unwavering eyes. "If you believe Jesus is God's only Son and the only way to salvation, then we believe the same."

Michael stared at him in silence. He had been around too many distrustful people to believe someone just because he said the right words. "Your necklace betrays you," Michael coldly replied.

"They all do. I hand-etched each one. Only thing, they don't have a cross on the back like mine." Michael was silent, not knowing what to say. "Sometimes we're forced to do things we don't want to," the old man continued. "But we make the most of it."

"So you're a prisoner, too?"

"I'm supposedly dead." His eyes became distant, yet not hateful. "They wanted me to work for them. When I refused, they staged my death, brought me here, and put me to work. I was a jeweler by trade." Speaking about his occupation in past tense made it clear that he found no joy in what he was forced to do. "I also help the cook. It gives me some freedom. Sometimes I help pick up supplies in town."

Michael remembered back to the jeep ride. "You were alone in the truck when I got on—couldn't you have escaped?"

"Maybe. But God's called me to work here."

"Called you here?" Michael asked incredulously.

"Son," the old man said gently, "God has a purpose in everything."

"But you've given up your life," Michael said, unable to comprehend the man's sacrifice.

The old man picked up his bucket and looked down at Michael, his eyes sincere. "I was on the front line in World War II. Killed two Japanese soldiers. I'm not proud of that, but we knew the enemy and we did what had to be done for the sake of peace. This war is different. It's subtle, and if there's no one in the foxhole except yourself—you're doomed. I hope you have God, Michael. Or more important, I hope God has you." He paused. "You say I've given up my life . . . I say I'm just beginning to find it." A moment later he was gone.

Michael stared at the door for a moment, the old man's words repeating over and over in his head. Then he lifted the sandwich to his mouth. The bread was soft, the meat thick. He was ravenous, but somehow he felt compelled to lay the food down and fold his hands.

"God, I don't understand why I'm here," he whispered. "I hate this place. I hate these people. I'm hurting. I've pleaded again and again for you to show me a way out." He took a ragged breath. "I don't understand this man. I feel empty and full of hate. I could never be like him." Feeling anything other than resentment turned things upside down. It went against his nature—his sense of logic. He struggled with the idea. "Never," he cried out, "never will I be thankful for this!"

A tear rolled down his face and he cried. He cried over his situation, cried out his pain, cried over wrong decisions, cried that he wasn't like the old man. Finally, out of weariness and an unrelenting force, he managed a prayer of gratitude for the water and the sandwich, the old man, and a mattress. But being thankful for being here was something he could not do.

Twenty-four

"There's a two-day seminar I'm supposed to attend," John told Marissa as they closed up one evening. "I can't go. But you'd enjoy it."

"Does that translate into an invitation or am I being sent?"

John smiled artfully. "Depends on what your answer is."

"When is it?" Marissa said, waving cigarette smoke out of her eyes. John had held true to his promise about not smoking in the office, but it was after hours. Apparently he felt entitled.

"Tomorrow. In Kona. Just take a cab to the airport."

"Thanks for the advance notice."

John chuckled. "I would wish you luck on finding a one-night stand, but I suppose you don't do things like that."

"Why? Because I'm a Christian?"

"That and you're waiting for something better."

"You think monogamy's better?" Marissa asked, surprised by his comment.

"I'm losing my kids, my house, my money—divorce is a royal pain. And now I think I've just met one of those fatal attraction cases. She won't let me break it off."

"Didn't you forget to mention AIDS?"

John shrugged. "We're all going to die sometime."

"Now that's an attitude," Marissa said as she reached for her blazer. Then, remembering what was in the pocket, she pulled out a thin paperback copy of *Mere Christianity* and tossed it on his desk. "I was going to let Lynn borrow this, but I'll let you read it first. Tell me what you think."

John picked up the book. "Does this mean lunch next week?"

"No, but if you read the whole thing, I'll buy you a box of those sickening sweet mocha chocolates you love so much."

"You know," John said, gazing appraisingly at her, "I think you're good for me. A little caloric, but good."

Marissa smiled as she walked out of the office. A different side of John was emerging, revealing a warmth that seemed almost human.

In the break room, Marissa spun the dial on her padlock, wondering if keeping her locker instead of using the office closet had helped one iota in playing down her promotion. She still felt friction between the others, and when Lynn walked in, Marissa pushed her travel document inside the locker, not wanting to tell her about the trip.

"Hi, Lynn. Busy tonight?"

"It's about par for a Tuesday. What's new with you?"

"Oh, same old thing," Marissa said, but as she turned, the travel document slid out and fell to the floor, John's handwriting clearly legible on the cover.

"Same old thing, huh?" Lynn said as Marissa quickly retrieved the packet.

"It's just a seminar," Marissa murmured sheepishly, but she knew Lynn worked long hours for less money, and two days in a hotel would be a nice vacation for her.

"Where's it at?"

"I think John said Luana something. It's on the big island."

"Must be Luana Hale. That place used to be ritzy. I heard it's not that great now."

"Wonderful." Marissa grabbed her purse and sweater and swung the locker door closed. "So I'll be killing cockroaches in a hotel room for two days."

"Right," Lynn said. "Well, at least bring me back a shower cap and some soap."

Marissa quickly agreed, relieved that Lynn's good nature came shining through.

❧   ❧   ❧   ❧

Wearing a business suit again felt good. She tipped the cab driver with her usual generosity, then cringed, remembering the few dollars she had in her wallet. She may have looked like an executive again—even felt like one—but in reality, the cabbie probably made more money than she did.

The letter Donald had sent her through the Thibedeauxes yesterday came to mind as she walked to the airport gate. In so many words—most of which were replete with legal jargon—Donald stated that if she didn't come back to work within ten days, her employment with Jonah Stevens was terminated. She had circled the tenth day on her wall calendar with a red marker and then stared at it, feeling hollow and depressed, unsure about what to do. Maybe a couple days away from everything was what she needed. Not having to go to the "Power for Success" class was another plus. She hadn't gotten any closer to finding Michael, and she despised the lectures and Steve's penetrating stares.

However, there was the opportunity to attend a retreat at the end of the course. One location was on Maui and the other was in Las Vegas. Michael's trip to Las Vegas immediately came to mind, and Marissa felt there must be some connection. She would have to hang in until the end.

As Marissa boarded the plane, a familiar voice called her name. Marissa looked over and saw Spencer, his blue eyes twinkling. An unexpected warmth surged through her and her eyes widened.

"So you're going to visit the volcanoes, too?" Spencer asked.

"Yeah," she replied, his smile immediately buoying her mood. "Volcanic managers. I'm going to a seminar."

Spencer's eyebrows rose. "First a banquet, then a seminar.

Maybe I should get a job as a hostess.''

"Maybe you should," Marissa said with amusement in her eyes as she moved on down the aisle.

Minutes after takeoff, Spencer slipped into the vacant seat next to her. "So what's new? You didn't look real happy when you walked on board."

"I don't know." Marissa sighed. "I was just thinking about home."

"Can I help?" Spencer offered.

Marissa shook her head. "Jonah Stevens just gave me an ultimatum. Either I return to work in ten days or my job is history."

"What are you going to do?"

"Run away to a seminar for a few days and think about it."

Spencer nodded. "A logical choice. You'll have plenty of time, too. This one isn't that interesting."

Marissa looked at him suspiciously. "Don't tell me you're going to the same seminar."

"Okay, I won't."

"You knew John was sending me to this?"

"I plead the fifth."

Marissa smiled and shook her head, but inside she was excited about spending two days with Spencer. It appeared he didn't mind, either.

"I need to ask you something," Marissa said a moment later. "What state of mind were you in when you hired John? Or were you on a mental vacation that day?"

Spencer laughed. "John's one in a million, isn't he? Womanizer, procrastinator—he doesn't even make it in to work everyday."

"I find no humor in it. Maybe it's because I have to work for him and you don't."

"John used to be an excellent manager and family man."

Marissa shook her head. "I don't think we're talking about the same guy."

"No, really, he was. He took over the restaurant when it was an okay place to eat and transformed it into one of the finest on the island. Then something happened. Mid-life crisis . . . something. I'm waiting to see if he rides it out. I feel like the Regency owes him something." He paused. "Say, I heard about your computer skills. I'm impressed."

"Well, don't be. It was only a simple spreadsheet."

"Aren't you happy about the promo?"

"I should be. Of course, Administrative Assistant positions are a dime a dozen."

"But you needed the dime, right?" She read the respect in his eyes as though he knew what she had left behind at Jonah Stevens.

"Right," she said, leaning her head on the headrest, trying not to think about the date circled in red on her calendar.

꙲   ꙲   ꙲   ꙲

"How about going for a walk?" Spencer said when they met later that evening.

"What? And pass up the open bar?" Marissa said in mock consternation. She looked at him almost critically. "I don't think I've ever seen you drink."

"I'll have an occasional beer now and then, but that's about it." Spencer directed her past priceless art collections and through an open-air courtyard toward the pristine beach. "Believe it or not, I used to get drunk in junior high."

"Junior high?" Marissa looked at him. "That's bordering on juvenile delinquent."

Spencer nodded. "My dad thought so, too, so he made me an offer. If I didn't drink another drop until I graduated from high school, he promised he'd teach me to fly." Spencer smiled. "We both held true to our promises."

"Your dad was pretty smart."

"He was," Spencer said.

When they reached the beach, Marissa paused to pull off her shoes. The slight breeze ruffled her cotton skirt and blouse. "So you go to this meeting every year?"

"It's kind of hard to pass up being pampered at a five-star hotel," he said, stopping to wait for her. "Are you going to try the mud bath, milk bath, or a combination of both?"

Marissa laughed out loud, thinking back to Lynn's comment. "Someone told me the hotel wasn't that great."

"Who?" Spencer said as they began walking again.

"Lynn. But actually, I told her the wrong name. I get all these Hawaiian names all jumbled up—hale, kale, whatever."

"The way I see it, you don't get much mixed up. So far, you've managed to make it to the top two business affairs in hotel management."

"And I've enjoyed them both very much," Marissa said with an infectious smile.

"This is what we get to take a ride on tomorrow," Spencer said, motioning toward a large catamaran. "They take us way down the Kona coast and then back. It's a great way to spend an afternoon."

As Spencer went on to describe last year's voyage, Marissa caught sight of a man in the distance standing under one of the outdoor torchlights. Something about him was familiar, causing a wave of apprehension to sweep through her. She kept up the light conversation with Spencer as she threw furtive glances the man's direction. Finally he turned. Marissa's stomach clenched tight when she recognized the thick frame, slicked-back hair, and bulbous nose. Uncle Hiram.

A moment later another man joined Hiram and began talking with him. Something about him was familiar, too. When the second man turned around and motioned Hiram to walk down the beach with him, Marissa stared, unbelieving, at Steve Porter. Her heart began to pound hard and she caught her breath sharply.

After hearing her catch her breath, Spencer said, "I know you have your mind set that you don't like it, but you have to try it tomorrow."

Marissa looked back to him. "I'm sorry. Try what?"

"Snorkeling," Spencer said. "What I've been talking about for the past five minutes."

Marissa nodded, but she could only think of Hiram and Steve. Could their own uncle be involved with Michael's disappearance? Was it his voice she had overheard on the club's lanai? Accusing him of something criminal made her feel like a traitor to her family. And yet, what was Hiram doing there with Steve? Planning another abduction? This time her own?

Marissa pulled her thoughts from such speculations, trying to assess her situation. Hiram and Steve were walking her way— and soon they'd be close enough to recognize her. There simply wasn't time enough to get back to the secluded hotel courtyard. Besides, Spencer might call out her name if she grabbed his hand and hurried him back. There was only one place to hide.

"Let's go wading," she spontaneously told Spencer, heading toward the surf. Spencer hesitated, as if considering his business shirt and slacks. But a moment later he kicked off his shoes and followed her lead.

"So you've turned into a mermaid?" Spencer said with a laugh, oblivious to her predicament.

"Right," Marissa agreed with a playful smile as she turned around in the knee-deep water. But her smile soon disappeared. She had hoped to be shrouded in darkness, but the row of restaurant torches lit up the water, even this far out. Fearing the men would look her way, Marissa moved close to Spencer, using him to block their view.

"I don't know what you have in mind," Spencer said, wrapping his arms around her, "but I'm liking this part."

Marissa looked into Spencer's eyes ready to make up an explanation, but the warmth of his body against her own drew unexpected emotions, and she found herself undeniably attracted.

The kiss was as natural as the ocean's next swell, and Marissa reveled in Spencer's exhilarating nearness. But afterward, held in his solid embrace, she was stirred out of her romantic fervor when she remembered Hiram and Steve. She lifted her head and looked the direction they had been walking. To her relief she saw them just as they turned up a walkway between two hotels.

"I liked that." Spencer's voice was low as he pulled away. "I've been wanting to tell you—" Spencer paused when he saw her staring over his shoulder.

As soon as Marissa saw which of the two hotels Hiram walked into, she quickly looked back to Spencer. But it was too late.

"Gawking at other guys while you're holding me isn't real romantic," Spencer said, dropping his arms from her shoulders.

"I wasn't looking at anyone, I was watching—" Marissa's words faded and there was an inept silence as Spencer waited for an answer she wasn't willing to give.

"Why don't you call me when you're done playing games," he finally said as he waded out of the water.

Marissa stared after him, angry over her inability to tell the truth but even more angry over his kissing her when he already had a girlfriend.

"Should I let Sheila know the game you're playing?" she threw back. Spencer paused for a moment, his back to her, but then he snatched up his shoes from the shore and kept walking.

Marissa followed Spencer's fading silhouette with her eyes, regretting her situation, her sarcastic words—even the attraction she had for him. *Maybe it's for the best,* she thought as she waded out of the water. She had work to do. Wringing out her skirt hem with determination and smoothing back her hair, Marissa made her way toward the nearby hotel. This man who she called uncle had better have some answers.

Twenty-five

Marissa paused in the shadow of the lounge door and scanned the patrons until she found Hiram perched on a barstool, alone and drinking straight shots. Apparently he hadn't quit drinking as he had told his sister. She found a table near the back, feeling conspicuous in her wet skirt. No one else seemed to notice.

"I'd like to buy that man in the striped shirt and tie another of whatever he's drinking," Marissa told the cocktail waitress, nodding to Hiram. "Tell him it's from Marissa."

When the drink was delivered, Marissa watched Hiram lean over to the waitress as if asking her to repeat her message. Then he turned around, his eyes nervously searching the bar. Great agitation filled his expression when he recognized her. He downed the remains of his drink in one gulp and scurried out the door. Marissa held tight to her courage and followed.

She caught sight of him as he turned down the first hallway in the lobby and then disappeared out an exit door. Hurrying down the street after him, she saw him dart into a heavily populated arcade. Working her way through the crowd, Marissa's anger and frustration grew. She was in no mood for a chase. She would find him and he would talk, she told herself determinedly.

Beeping sounds and flashes of digitized light reflected from the player's faces as she searched for a stocky man who was engaged in his own game of flight. At first she walked by the video machine he was pressed up against, but his shirt caught her eye and she turned back.

"I think we need to play a game or two," she said, sitting down on a plastic stool, trapping him between herself and the wall. She regarded the busily moving battle scene on the screen and then gave him a hard look.

Hiram stared back. "You look like your mom," he finally said.

Marissa surveyed him, noting the lines on his face were deeper than what she remembered, the pores on his swollen nose even larger. The smell of cheap liquor permeated his breath and his clothing. "What are you doing in Hawaii?" Marissa inquired, fishing coins out of her wallet.

"I'm on business."

"Oh, really? I didn't think accountants traveled much."

"It's a perk. I have clients who live here."

"Wait a minute. Didn't you and Michael and I have a meeting set up for tomorrow?" Marissa said, her hand poised above the machine's coin slot. "Tomorrow is the fifteenth, isn't it? Now, how could we all sign off on the will with you being here?"

"When I called your office to cancel, they said you were over here."

"No, they didn't," Marissa said, turning fiery eyes on him. "They don't know where I am." Hearing him speak now brought her to the horrible realization that it had been his voice she had overheard on the lanai. "My being on this island is no surprise to you," she stated forcefully. "You'd better tell me what's going on."

"I don't know what you're talking about."

"Quit lying. I heard your conversation with the woman in Maui. You needed to find me—your client. Well, here I am. What do you want?"

Hiram looked away from her to the bullets racing across the screen as the machine played a game of atomic destruction against itself. "You better talk to me," Marissa threatened, her voice rising.

"Lower your voice," Hiram whispered. Tiny beads of sweat were forming on his forehead and he glanced around nervously. "Look, I got into something over my head and now I—" He pulled at the tie around his neck. "They own me."

"Who's they?"

"Vanus, Ekvar, White and Hall—they have a lot of different names. Own a lot of things. I just do their books and keep my mouth shut."

"Ekvar? So you know about Michael's investment?"

Hiram's eyes burned defiantly. "He got into that mess himself. I had nothing to do with it. When I saw his check, it was too late." Hiram looked around again before continuing. "They research everybody," he said, his voice barely audible, "always looking for a deep pocket. They found out about the inheritance money."

"They already have most of it."

"They want all of it," Hiram said, wiping the sweat off his forehead with a trembling hand. "Look, I can't be seen with you. They've killed for less."

"Killed? What about Michael? Where are they keeping him?"

"Keeping him?" Hiram asked, obviously surprised by her comment.

"Yes. He's been missing for weeks now."

"Oh no, that's . . . not Michael . . . I didn't—" For a moment remorse enveloped Hiram's face, but an instant later the fear returned with even more domination.

"Marissa, don't mess with these people," he whispered hoarsely. "They play for keeps. Just give them what they want." Spinning her chair around, he bolted like a cornered rat and disappeared out a side door.

Twenty-six

When Marissa returned from the airport, five messages, all concerning work, were waiting on her answering machine. "I've been waitressing *and* playing manager," Lynn complained via the machine. "John has only shown his face around here long enough to make the deposits and then leave."

Marissa looked at her watch and sighed. It was seven in the evening and she was tired. Spencer hadn't talked to her all day, and she spent every break from the seminar next to a phone asking hotel clerks if they had a Hiram Wells listed. She'd come up empty.

Leaving her packed suitcase, Marissa walked to the restaurant and worked straight through to closing. "John owes us both one," she confided to Lynn as they headed to the bank of elevators. "I'm exhausted. I hope I assigned everyone the right shifts, otherwise this next week is going to be chaotic."

"Couldn't be worse than when you office people were gone." Lynn punched the elevator button impatiently, the contempt in her voice unmistakable.

It was obvious that the small gift Marissa bought for Lynn on the big island wouldn't help soothe the difficulties she'd had these last two days. Well, Marissa thought, she'd had enough of everything and everyone today. She was tired and didn't have the energy to "talk things through." Hopefully everything would be better tomorrow.

Surprisingly, it was. Flowers arrived at the office the next afternoon with a card attached, "Sorry and thank you. John." At
first Marissa thought John had gotten the business address
mixed up with one of his girlfriends', but that afternoon he came
in wearing a tie and confirmed the benevolent gesture.

"I see you got the flowers."

"Thank you, but I think they should go to Lynn."

John frowned. "The prima donna?"

"Don't you think that's a little harsh? She's one of your better waitresses, you know. I'd cut her some slack." Marissa decided not to remind him that because he hired on looks, his
turnover was horrendous and Lynn had to spend a lot of time
training.

"That doesn't give her license to use the office whenever she
feels like it," John retorted.

"What do you mean?"

"I've found her in here a few times. When I asked her what
she was doing, she nearly came unglued. Told me that you said
she could take her break in here whenever she wanted. I knew
you wouldn't tell her that."

"How would you know what I'd say?"

"You're smart, and that wouldn't be a smart thing to do."

Marissa didn't let his back-door compliment sway her, and
she continued to push the point. "Still, Lynn covered for you
for two days. I wouldn't lynch her for just sitting in the office a
few minutes."

"She didn't have to cover. I asked Don to take care of
things."

"The busboy?"

"Yeah. He's bright—has plans to go to college."

"Whatever," Marissa mumbled, handing John the folder
they'd given her at the seminar. "I organized my notes for you
on the flight back."

As John started reading, he pulled a pack of cigarettes out
of his pocket and fished for his lighter.

"A promise is a promise," Marissa said, picking up the pack

and tossing it to the far side of the desk.

John laid the report down and leaned back. "Ah yes. You are back," he bantered with a hint of cynicism. Then he said, "I read your Christianity book."

"What did you think?"

"That you want to convert me."

"God does the converting."

John sighed. "The low key approach, huh? Well, I have a question for you. Can God make a rock heavier than he can lift?"

Marissa shook her head in frustration. "If that's what you got out of the book, forget it."

John laughed. "So you're giving up on me?"

"I might be, but God's more patient." Marissa glanced at her watch and then stood. "I'd love to talk more, but I have to get to my class."

"Say, how did you like the seminar? Did you fall in love?"

"Yeah," Marissa said as she paused at the door. "With a pair of shoes and I bought 'em."

☙ ☙ ☙ ☙

Renae had a meeting and couldn't make it to class, so Marissa again rented a car. Afterward, she drove to the condo, ate a quick dinner, then hurried across the parking lot. She wanted to at least be on time since she'd missed the last two classes.

As if it were planned, Spencer drove up and parked next to her as she was unlocking the car door. "Bought a car?" he asked as he climbed out.

"No. It's a rental. The kind you get when you bring in a coupon." She hoped some light conversation would cover her awkwardness. They hadn't talked to each other since the incident in Kona.

"It's not that bad," Spencer said. Their eyes met and held.

"Look, about the other night . . ." Marissa paused. "I'm sorry."

"So am I," Spencer quickly offered. There was a silence.

"Well, I better get going," Marissa said, zipping her belt bag. "I'm supposed to be at Maka Beach in fifteen minutes."

"Okay," Spencer said, but instead of leaving, he hesitated. Something in his eyes made her pause, as well. It was as if they both wanted to say something, but neither did, and Marissa drove away trying not to think about what it was that affected her every time she saw him.

Marissa was late. Again. Classmates were sitting on the floor in circles of six drawing with crayons. Marissa cringed when Steve walked toward her with one of his plastic smiles.

"Here's a place for you," he told her, motioning toward a group of five. After she sat down, he handed her a crayon. "We're using paper and crayons to better explore our feelings— to bring out our inner child. Draw something that would make you happy and fulfilled."

"That's easy," Marissa said. The others in the group looked over, curious. Marissa drew a vertical line down and intersected it with a shorter line. "Jesus died on the cross for me. He loves me, and He'll be with me always—even after I die. Knowing that gives me all the joy and fulfillment I need."

Steve's chuckle mocked her words. "God is a transformational idea," his soothing voice reassured. "Seeking a higher source of goodness is quite acceptable. Over time you'll see fulfillment has many levels." He stepped away and raised his voice. "We have five more minutes and then we'll talk about how to claim this fulfillment."

His comment angered Marissa, but arguing would bring about nothing good so she remained quiet. At least she'd had the opportunity to express her beliefs. Moments later Marissa listened to Steve instruct them to find a mat and lie down. As everyone shuffled off toward a mat, Marissa contemplated leaving, finding the whole scenario a bit disturbing. But somehow she felt compelled to stay. *If I don't*, she reasoned, *all my time attending this class will be wasted.* She found a mat and lay on her back like the others. She had to admit that the cool vinyl felt good since the room had been especially warm that evening.

Steve told them to close their eyes, breathe deeply, and visualize themselves on a spacecraft taking them to another planet. Once there, they were told to look back to earth and feel a sense of oneness with the cosmos. Despite her aversion to his words, Marissa thought she would at least close her eyes. It had been a busy day at work, and she could use a respite.

"Release your anger," Steve repeated softly.

Well, I can agree with that, she thought to herself, remembering her pent-up emotions. And, amazingly, she did seem to feel a floating sensation when he mentioned the word. *Not anything wrong with floating*, she thought. There were more repeated phrases and background music or words . . . she couldn't quite separate them. Her head felt lighter.

Steve began telling them to empty their minds bit by bit and then consider their inner potential, to think of themselves as a divine entity, free of guilt and iniquity. Her eyes flicked open. Now, there was something wrong with that. As a Christian, she was to fill her mind with the knowledge of God—not empty it— and sin would be in her life until she was with Jesus. She glanced around. Everyone else was lying still, listening to the easy-to-accept, feel-good phrases. She was beginning to understand more about what the power was in the "Power for Success" classes and who had the control. She endured the rest of the mat time by calling up memorized Bible verses in her mind, all the while realizing that everyone else in the room was playing with fire.

In a few minutes the lights that she hadn't noticed dim became brighter, and Steve instructed them to put away their mats and they were dismissed. Today's session was extremely different from the previous classes. She wondered if the others felt the same way, or if they had been subtly led to this point in the last two sessions. She wished Renae were there. She picked up her books, wanting to leave immediately, then remembered her promise to pick up notes for Renae.

"You're missing some handouts, no doubt," Steve commented as she approached the front of the room after class. His eyebrows looked heavier than before, his eyes colder. Marissa wished she had asked for the paper work during the break.

"Yes. I was out of town," she said nervously. "And I wanted to pick up tonight's notes for Renae."

Steve nodded thoughtfully. "Have you gotten something out of the class?" he inquired, his voice so smooth it was irritating.

"It's been enlightening," Marissa said, glancing down at his watchband and quickly meeting his eyes again. He noticed.

"Are you familiar with the insignia?" he asked, motioning to his watch. His eyes asked the question more than his words. They pierced and dug, but Marissa remained invincibly calm.

"No. Maybe you could explain."

Steve smiled coolly. "The dragon represents power—power over any obstacle. The rainbow encircling means tranquillity, joy, and fulfillment. Just what we've been discussing in class."

"How would you get a watch like that?"

"Ahhh. Too many questions, too soon. Wait until next week, and I'll tell you and the others." He looked back to the podium. "Now for the handouts you missed." He searched through a stack of papers and then picked up another. "I thought I had them right here." He appeared extremely organized, and Marissa found it hard to believe he would misplace anything.

"I can wait until next time," Marissa said, glancing behind her and noticing only three classmates in the room. Scenes from the parking lot flashed to her memory, and she didn't want to take the chance of ending up alone with him again.

"No, I'll find them," he told her, reaching toward a stack of papers he hadn't touched. "In fact, here they are."

Marissa accepted the papers with a weak thank-you and turned around. His eyes had been calculating, as if he knew something she didn't. All she wanted to do was leave.

"Wait," Steve said. "We had two handouts on session six."

Marissa reluctantly turned back.

"Here's the other one," he said. "I hope all the pages are here." Marissa silently suffered as he counted the sheets and finally handed them to her. "Thanks for waiting."

At that moment she knew something wasn't right. His eyes weren't shifty, but content. She turned abruptly, and fear pounded in her chest when she realized the door leading out of the room was shut and she was the only student left.

Get out, get out, her mind silently screamed. She hurried to the door and turned the handle, but it wouldn't open. Shifting her notebook to the other arm, she tried again, harder. She felt Steve's eyes stabbing her in the back. Panic constricted her throat when she heard him approaching and she quickly turned to face him.

"You shouldn't have taken this course," he said, his voice hard and not at all like the one he used in class. "You're meddling where you don't belong."

Marissa took a deep breath. "I just want my brother."

"Mike wants to be where he is. He joined our group voluntarily."

"I'd rather ask him that personally," Marissa said, her eyes frantically searching for a way of escape.

"Maybe that can be arranged," Steve said, producing an evil smile as he lunged for her.

Turning her notebook flat, Marissa shoved it against his throat and bolted for the side door, pushing a chair over on the way. Steve cursed as he turned for her and stumbled over the chair. He scrambled to his feet a moment later.

Marissa fled down a dimly lit hall toward a lighted exit sign, where she threw herself at the closed door. It flew open, striking the back wall and sounding like the boom of a cannon. A concrete stairwell faced her, and her steps echoed raucously as she followed them down. She nearly fell on the first turnaround and whimpered like a small child as she steadied herself and continued down the next two flights.

Another exit light shone at the bottom. With arms extended, she leaped over the last two steps and pushed against the bar.

But the door wouldn't open. She tried again and again, but the metal door remained a two-inch barrier between her and freedom. Steve's laughter rang barbarously from the doorway above, confirming her fear. Her escape route wasn't one at all.

"You and your brother have a lot in common," Steve shouted, his words ricocheting down to her. Then he laughed again. "See you in the morning." The door thudded shut and all was silent.

Marissa rubbed her bare arms and stood at the bottom of her concrete prison. Steve was all the evil things she first thought him to be. He must have abducted Michael, or at least lured him away, and now Steve had her in his talons. There was no concern for the inner child in this place. She crept up the gritty stairs and tried the door, even though she knew it would be locked. Sinking down on a step, Marissa searched through her belt pack. Nothing to pick a door with, even if she knew how. Would this just be a warning for her, or was this the first day of her abduction?

Almost like a physical blow, reality hit and her mind dredged up lurid ways Steve could deal with her. Hugging her knees, she closed her eyes, trying not to doubt God's providence. "Lord God, I know you're here with me," she whispered. "You know these people and their evil ways, but you are stronger. Jesus, you are victorious. I know you can work a miracle. Please, God, open my eyes to a way of escape." Then she hesitated, ending her prayer with words that were usually easy to say, but this time were extremely difficult. "But if this is your will, Lord, help me be strong."

Opening her eyes, though still hugging her body defensively, she sat still, listening. Only the sound of distant traffic. Then the feel of something foreign on her neck made her jump and a giant spider fell to the floor. Repulsed, Marissa quickly stood and frantically brushed her hair and clothes. She peered up at the ceiling and then around her, wondering how many other insects considered this their home.

Still wiping at her shoulders, but not so vigorously, Marissa looked to the wall. A small opening caught her eye. It was only six inches by eight inches—an impossible escape route—but she discovered that if she stood on one step and leaned against the wall, she could see past some bushes to the bottom half of what looked to be a garbage dumpster and a dark alley beyond. Trying to forget about the creeping insects, she put her face near the opening and called out, tentatively at first.

"Hello?" she said. "Can anybody hear me?" An industrial part of town, the buildings were far apart and empty at this time of night, but she continued to call out louder and louder, again and again, hoping a night watchman or security guard patrolling one of the other buildings would hear her.

Finally, after her voice had become hoarse and she was chilled from leaning against the cold, damp wall, she left her post and walked up and down the stairs, trying to get warm. She'd dropped her sweater somewhere along the chase, and her short-sleeved T-shirt and lightweight slacks provided little warmth.

Pausing in a patch of moonlight, she checked her watch. It was past midnight. What time did Steve mean when he said "morning"? Halfway up the steps, she heard something. She stopped and listened. The sound of a vehicle.

With renewed energy, she went to the opening and looked out. All she could see was the bottom half of a car driving slowly by. "Help me," she yelled. "Stop!"

When the car continued her yells grew frantic. For a moment she thought the car was going to turn the corner and disappear. Then suddenly it stopped. She saw a pair of legs swing out of the car, walk a few steps, then pause.

"Over here," she yelled. "Behind the dumpster." Marissa's heart pounded. Had Steve sent someone to finish her off? Had she just led him over?

The bushes parted and a face appeared.

Twenty-seven

Even in the dimness, Marissa recognized the face immediately. "Spencer!" she cried with a ragged sob, reaching through the opening and clutching his hand.

"Marissa, what are you doing down there?" Spencer's face displayed a mixture of concern and shock. "You're cold," he said, rubbing her hand. "Are you hurt?"

She shook her head, suddenly beginning to shiver uncontrollably. "He's trapped me down here and he's coming back soon. Please get me out."

"Who's 'he'?" Spencer demanded, acting as though he would settle the score with whoever did this to her.

Marissa looked at him miserably. "Steve Porter."

"Porter?" Spencer looked at her as if her answer didn't make sense. But a second later he seemed to dismiss the thought. "Never mind. We just need to get you out of there."

"There's an exit door down there," Marissa said, motioning with her head. "It's locked. I can't get it open."

"I'll go look at it." Spencer squeezed her hand, then disappeared around the corner. She heard noises near the door, and a moment later he was at the opening again.

"I hate to leave you here, but I need to get some tools. Hopefully it won't take long. Here." He unzipped his jacket and stuffed it between the bars. "Put this on."

She pulled the jacket in only to reach for his hand again.

"Please hurry," she said as tears welled up in her eyes. "I'm . . . I'm scared."

"I will. I promise." Spencer gave her one last look before he let go of her hand and hurried to his car.

Only after Marissa watched the car's taillights move away and disappear did she make a move to put on the coat. The too-large jacket smelled of Spencer's clean, fresh scent, and she sank down on the step directly under the window, buried her face in the collar, and prayed.

Minutes dragged by. Marissa listened to the night insects and an occasional car engine on a faraway road. Her head ached from physical and mental tenseness, but she wasn't shivering quite so hard. The coat and hope of Spencer's return warmed her.

As she looked at the wall straight ahead for the umpteenth time, something caught her eye. Faint letters, spotlighted by the moon, were scratched at knee level. No one walking down the steps would probably notice them—only someone like herself who had spent time there . . . at night . . . with the moonlight spilling in. With trembling limbs she knelt down and carefully studied the cool, damp wall. *Montana 3 Kansas 2*. Marissa's eyes scanned the words slowly. A game's score or . . . M-I-K-E. The nickname Michael hated conveyed so much.

"How much time did you spend down here, little brother?" she whispered, running her fingers over the letters as a gamut of emotions washed over her. "Did you want to come here, or did you get caught up in Steve's lies?" Suddenly Marissa thought that it didn't matter either way. All she wanted to do was see her brother again—apologize for being so caught up in their petty differences and this time be there when he needed someone to listen.

"I'm going to find you, Michael." Her voice was husky. "I'm getting closer and I'm not going to give up."

Twenty minutes later the sound of a car engine brought Marissa back to the opening. Footsteps approached and her heart pounded. Was it Spencer or Steve?

"Marissa?" Spencer called softly.

"Yes," she said, relief in her voice.

"I'm going to cut the door," Spencer said, setting down two long metal bottles, a welding mask, and a torch. "How far can you move away?"

"I can go up a flight of stairs."

"Good," he said, pulling on a pair of heavy gloves. "Wait there."

Marissa heard the acetylene torch fire and saw the reflection of sparks as they cascaded down the metal door. At the same time she saw a slit of light shine near the bottom of the upper door. Someone was inside the building.

Covering her eyes, she moved toward the lower metal door. Spencer just had to hurry. When the door clicked open, she darted out and Spencer hugged her hard. "Somebody just drove up in the front," he whispered in her ear. "Grab a bottle and run to the car."

Fueled by adrenaline, they both ran toward the car and in less than a minute, they were speeding down the alley with Marissa twisting in her seat, looking behind. "You okay?" Spencer said when they reached the main road.

Marissa nodded as she faced front again, but she kept her hands clasped tight together and didn't talk until they were blocks farther from the building. "I shouldn't have risked going to class alone tonight," she said, as much to herself as to Spencer.

"You're taking one of Steve's classes?"

She nodded woodenly and then passed on the information she had so fiercely guarded. "My brother has been missing for over a month and Steve knows where he is."

"Missing?" Spencer turned his head sharply to look at her. "How do you connect Steve with your brother?"

"I wasn't sure of much of anything until I saw my uncle Hiram in Kona—during our wade in the water. That's who I was looking at on the beach." Marissa's eyes cautiously pleaded for understanding and forgiveness. His warm gaze seemed to offer it. "I followed him afterward and discovered he works as Steve's accountant. Hiram's terrified over what he's involved in and won't say much. They seem to keep him in the dark, but he knew Michael invested in one of Steve's companies."

"Investing is one thing, being missing is another." Spencer paused, trying to piece together the information. "So you think Steve took him here? Abducted him?"

Marissa shrugged hopelessly. "They have most of our inheritance. All we have left is the house. I think Michael knows too much about their business—or was once involved in it." She looked out the side window, trying not to think of her brother working for Steve.

"I'd like to help," Spencer said, reaching over and squeezing her hand. "What's your next step?"

"I don't know." Her words were barely audible.

When they finally arrived at their condominium complex, Spencer flipped on the entry lights in his unit, tossed his keys on an end table, and walked into the kitchen.

"I heard your stomach growling in the car," Spencer observed, pulling a carton of eggs and some ham out of the refrigerator. "So I think some food wouldn't be a bad idea."

Still wearing Spencer's jacket, Marissa walked past the blues and creams of his furniture, a rowing machine, and an extensive collection of CDs, then sat across from him on a barstool. She watched as he cracked eggs into a stainless-steel bowl. "I owe you a lot," she finally said, not knowing exactly how to thank him for the risk he had taken tonight.

"I'm just glad I found you."

"How *did* you find me?"

"I—" he paused. "It's kind of embarrassing, but I listen for you to come home at night. For some reason I sleep a lot better."

Marissa watched him stir the eggs, profoundly comforted by his care. "That proves you're a true gentleman."

"It proves a lot more than that." He stopping stirring and looked over at her. "Just before our little swim in Kona, I was trying to tell you that Sheila and I aren't seeing each other anymore. Even before I met you, I knew the relationship wasn't right. I just needed a nudge. Being your friend helped me see that there's so much more to share with a Christian. I . . . I won't settle for less again."

He appeared relieved over her knowing and gave her a small smile. "Anyway," he said, popping some bread in the toaster, "when it started getting late, I remembered you mentioning Maka Beach. I drove out there thinking it would be a pretty long shot to find you and that I may be butting in where I didn't belong. But when I saw your car parked in front of a building with all the lights off, I got worried. I decided to drive around the building. That's when I heard you yelling."

"What about the welding equipment? How did you find it so quick?"

"Theo, my partner with the helicopter, has a garage about a few miles away. I was praying he still kept a key hidden in the back."

Marissa looked across the kitchen, recalling the evening in quick flashbacks. "It was a miracle," she said softly.

"Yeah, God still works those," Spencer said matter-of-factly.

Marissa focused again on Spencer, amazed over how close she felt to him.

"Better sit down," Spencer pronounced as he carried plates heaped with eggs, thick slices of ham, and buttered toast to the table. He went back for a handful of napkins and they sat down, each bowing their heads.

"Father," Spencer began, "we thank you for your protection tonight and how you worked everything out for us. Please give Marissa wisdom and peace about finding her brother. You know where he is. Protect him this very moment. We thank you for this food we're about to eat. Amen."

"Thank you," she said afterward. Their eyes held for a moment and Marissa felt an unspoken bond. She had never prayed with Donald—never shared this emotion.

"You're a good cook," Marissa said after she'd eaten more than she ever thought she could.

"Eggs are kind of hard to mess up, but I'll accept the compliment." He winked at her as he reached for another piece of toast. "You sure are hanging in there like a trooper."

"I don't have many options."

"I still don't understand how you linked Steve to all of this." Marissa cradled her coffee cup in her hands. "He wears a watch with the same insignia that was on a pendant Michael left in his apartment—the one I wouldn't let go of in the elevator."

Spencer looked at her in fascination as she put the pieces together for him. "But how did you know Michael was in Maui?"

"He left a coded note."

"Coded? As in James Bond?"

"More like James Bond Junior. My brother and I used a code when we were kids, and miraculously, we both remembered it."

Spencer waited a moment and then said, "Well, what is it? I mean, what's the code?"

"I've never told anyone," she said slowly.

"You don't trust me?"

"Of course I trust you. You just got me out of that dungeon. It's just that . . . Oh, it's nothing," she said, pushing the childhood promise of never telling from her thoughts.

Over another cup of coffee, she explained the code. Spencer leaned back and grinned. "That's pretty neat. Let's try a couple practice ones," he said and scribbled something on a note pad.

"Did we get our vowels mixed up?" Marissa said, looking over at Spencer when his clue didn't make sense.

"No. I spelled O-N-O."

Marissa raised her eyebrows.

"You were supposed to guess 'fish,' " Spencer said. "Ono is one of the most popular fish on the island. Now who's the one who can't decipher?"

Marissa didn't smile back. His teasing suddenly made her feel guilty about breaking her and Michael's childhood pact. "It's best if you know the other person well," she said quietly.

"And we don't?"

Marissa laid down her napkin and turned to look out the window at the lighted walkway and the deserted pavilion. This lightheartedness was useless, and her sharing more of herself, unwise. She knew better. "As soon as I find Michael, I'll be going back to Portland."

"To your job . . . or Donald?"

Tears stung her eyes. She probably didn't have either. There was an uncomfortable silence.

"Sounds like there are a lot of maybes in your life," Spencer stated, scooting back his chair and standing. "I know one thing, though. You're staying here tonight. I'll get some sheets and a blanket, and you can sleep on the couch."

Marissa didn't argue. She felt safe here.

Twenty-eight

*E*very few hours, Michael pulled himself up and stared at the seascape through the iron bars until the throbbing in his leg forced him back to the mattress. The three-by-two-foot scene of the world refreshed him. There was no peace in this place, no comfort in these cold walls, and yet ever since his clumsy prayer of gratitude over the sandwich, he felt a strange sense of solace. Was this Jesus' presence?

He closed his eyes in an effort to remember some of the Bible verses he and Marissa had memorized as kids, but they had been neglected too long. Even John 3:16—heralded at nearly every sporting event—was foggy after the sixth word. All those years of sitting in church, hearing the Bible read, claiming the promises . . . and he couldn't recite one verse. It was a sad commentary on his faith walk.

But a hope dawned when he thought of the songs. "Jesus loves me, this I know," he started weakly, remembering the words as he sang. Other songs began to flood his memory. "Zaccheus." "This Little Light of Mine." He felt victorious after singing the entire first verse of "Living for Jesus." And then he sang them all again, his spirit lifting.

The door opened in the middle of his weak and yet triumphant recital, and the old man slipped in. "I may be a little hard of hearing," he said with a twinkle in his eye, "but I always seem to hear singing."

Michael accepted the bottle of water and sandwich, feeling indebted to this old man for not only saving him physically but renewing him spiritually. "I owe my life to you," Michael said, his voice thick with emotion. "And I don't even know your name."

"My name's Gabriel."

"As in the angel?"

Gabriel smiled. "And you're Michael Tomsen, without the 'h.' "

"How did you know?"

Gabriel held Michael's gaze as if weighing a heavy decision. "A few of my friends have started a network to help people like you. It's undercover and very risky."

"You mean to help get me out?"

"You and the others."

Michael remembered back to the first time he had been in the cafeteria and the man had commented on the "other ex-convict."

"How many are there?" Michael asked, wanting to know and yet not wanting to know because he knew their agony.

"Two. One of them died a week ago."

"Died?"

Gabriel nodded. "He had a seizure. I couldn't help him." Gabriel's face wore a pained expression, as though he were still grieving the death.

"Were they abducted, too?"

Gabriel shook his head. "One was a reporter. They found him spying on the operation. The other was an ex-guard. He didn't want to work here anymore. He didn't realize that he lost his choice of livelihood when he accepted the lucrative wage the guards get."

Michael took in a labored breath. He, too, was someone who wouldn't do as they commanded. "When do they plan—"

A noise outside the room made them both freeze. When they didn't hear anything more for a full minute, Gabriel spoke softly and quickly. "It's best you don't know any more. What I need from you is a contact person. Someone who can help us on the outside. Someone you trust implicitly."

Every friend fell short of the requirement except one. "Marissa Tomsen," Michael said. "My sister."

Twenty-nine

*T*he next morning Spencer insisted on helping Marissa retrieve her rental car. She thanked him for the second time
as they walked into the hotel together.

"No problem," Spencer said. "Are you sure you even want
to work today?"

"I have to. John's out of town, and . . . well, I don't want
the hotel manager mad at me." She forced a smile that didn't
reach her eyes.

"Call me after work. I'll drive you home, okay?"

Marissa nodded as she walked on the waiting elevator.

"Hate to hit you with a customer first thing," Lynn told
Marissa as she walked to her office. "But there's a guy who
wants to talk to the person in charge. Probably a complaint. He
seems pretty keyed up. He's waiting over there." Lynn flicked
her wrist toward the cashier's podium, where a tall, wiry man
was looking at his watch.

"Thanks, Lynn."

Marissa took a deep breath. She'd handled only two of these,
and neither one had been enjoyable. *The customer's always right*,
she reminded herself. Pasting a smile on her face, she walked
over.

"My name is Marissa Tomsen," she said, holding out her
hand. "How can I help you?"

With a perfunctory handshake, he said, "I'd like to reserve

one of your best tables for a group of ten. I have no time to discuss details, so I've written down the particulars." He handed her an envelope. "Call me if you have questions."

"If you'll wait just a moment," Marissa began, "I'll check the calendar and then we—"

"I really don't have the time," the man said, edging away. "Just read the note and we'll get in touch." With that, he disappeared around the corner toward the bank of elevators.

Something about his firmness in leaving seemed odd and Marissa pulled out the note. *Be at The Seascape in one hour. We can help you find Michael.*

Marissa's heart beat wildly. Who was this man and how had he found her? Was he someone to be trusted or a part of Steve's entourage? She rushed to the elevator lobby, assertively excusing herself past several people and then searching the faces anxiously. He wasn't there.

Several people looked at her oddly as she walked back. So did the cashier. "The man forgot to leave his phone number," Marissa mumbled as she walked toward her office.

Exactly one hour later, Marissa walked into The Seascape, a tourist shop two blocks west of the hotel. An Omni theater was located in the back, and shows ran every two hours for forty minutes. Marissa read the sign and looked at her watch. The next show was to begin in five minutes. About a dozen people waited near the back.

Adrenaline pumping, she walked past them toward the far corner, paused, and then pretended to be shopping. She picked up a shell figurine. After her trembling fingers almost lost their grip on the expensive piece, she quickly returned it to the shelf and opted for something heavier. She reached for a paperweight, but drew back when she noticed a scorpion suspended in the hardened milarite. She tried not to connect the venomous arachnid with her situation. Finally she picked up a plastic hula doll.

"That's a nice scene, isn't it?" a voice said. The wiry man had appeared out of nowhere and was now standing next to her, admiring a tropical print hanging at eye level on the wall.

Marissa looked at the man briefly and then forced her eyes to the print, her heart hammering in her chest. "Yes, it is," she said woodenly.

"We know where Michael is," the man said softly.

"Where?" she whispered back.

"Too many lives are at stake. We can't tell you."

"Who's we?" Marissa asked, clutching the hula doll.

"Some of us have family in the same situation. Most of us are Christians."

"How do I know you're not part of Steve Porter's group?"

The man glanced down the aisle and then back to her. "Michael says he knows a code."

The simple sentence gave her the assurance of truth she needed, and she quickly said, "Is he all right?" She held her breath, waiting.

"He's injured and weak. They have him in a basement room, secluded, tight security. We don't know how he is intellectually."

"What do you mean?"

"Mind empowerment, psychotherapy—we don't know exactly what they've done. Recovery is up to family members."

Recovery, mind empowerment . . . Marissa felt nauseous. "I . . . I don't understand."

The man looked down at her, as if surprised. "Your brother is in a cult." The plastic stand cracked in her hands and the doll's body fell to the floor, though Marissa was unaware. "Our contacts will let us know when it's best to attempt a rescue," the man said in a barely audible voice.

"But you said he's sick, injured. Can't you get him out now?" The man appeared nervous when a woman paused for a moment at the end of the aisle, then walked on.

"Timing's not right," he said, edging away. "We'll contact you when it is. Until then, watch your back and don't talk." A moment later he pretended to see someone he knew outside the store, waved, and hurried out.

Marissa walked back to the hotel, closed the office door, and leaned against it. *A cult.* She took deep breaths, trying to think clearly. Had Michael given up his faith in God? Was he staring at a crystal or a rock trying to be transcended or understood? She walked across the office and stared unseeing at the scantily clad woman on John's calendar. Why hadn't Michael confided in her? Why hadn't she listened more and argued less? If only—

John's entrance startled her and she jumped. "My rendez-vous ended a little early," John said glibly. "She had to bail, so I—" he paused. "What's up? You look pale. Don't tell me you have that flu crud that's going around."

Marissa put her hand to her cheek. "I . . . I don't feel that great."

"Then go home. I don't want to catch it," John said. "Get some sleep. You'll be okay."

Sleep wasn't what she desired, but leaving was. John waited for Marissa to gather up her things and then he ushered her out the door, mumbling about getting a can of disinfectant from maid service.

Marissa walked off the elevator, her mind unable to stop thinking about Michael. She paused near a bank of phones, wanting to call Spencer, but not knowing if it was wise to drag him in any further.

"See, I didn't think you should have come in today," Spencer said, walking across the lobby toward her. "I just called up there and John said you were leaving—felt sick. I'll drive you home."

"Can we walk?" she said, nodding to the rear exit.

Spencer looked surprised. "On the beach?"

She nodded.

"I don't know." Spencer grinned. "We tried that before, remember?" When she didn't react, his smile faded. "What's wrong?"

Marissa looked behind them several times as they walked down the beach path, not liking the added onus of having to watch her back. "Someone contacted me," she finally announced, trying to keep her emotions at bay. "He told me that Michael's in a cult."

Spencer reached out and stopped her, concern on his face. "A cult? Who contacted you?"

"A man. He said he wants to help."

"And you believe him?"

"I don't have many options."

"Does he want money?" Spencer's lips thinned.

"He didn't mention a fee. He only said it wasn't safe to get Michael now, and that I'd just have to wait."

"Until?"

"He didn't say." Marissa looked out at the ever breaking surf, feeling Spencer's frustration about not being able to help her. She didn't know what to do herself. Nothing was clear—there were no road maps. But later that night, after she tossed in bed for what seemed like an eternity, she suddenly sat straight up. A puzzle piece fit. She picked up the phone.

"Spencer, can we talk?" Marissa's voice was quiet, yet excited.

"Yeah," he said huskily. "But it's—" She heard bedding rustling. "It's three in the morning."

"I know. Sorry. Can I come down?"

"Uhhh. Sure. Come on down."

Spencer let her in. His hair was tousled and he had on a wrinkled T-shirt and shorts. His breath smelled like toothpaste.

"I think I know where Michael is," Marissa said softly.

"They contacted you again?"

"No. I just put some things together."

"Okay," he said, trying to conceal a yawn as he motioned her over to the couch. "Tell me."

"Most cult members wear similar clothing, right?" Spencer rubbed his face and then nodded. "On your first airdrop, you know, the one you told me that a whole bunch of white material fell out of the ripped bags?" Spencer nodded. "Well, they could have been robes or shirts—some type of similar clothing."

"Or they could have been sheets for their guest rooms."

Spencer attempted to be realistic.

"I know, but there's other things that point to them, like the fact that the building is remote and you said they don't like motorized vehicles around. That would make the place easier to guard and they could keep close track of who came and went."

"I know you're anxious to find Michael, but there are lots of places like that on this island."

"Really? I would think that most people who own tourist places like roads so people can get there."

"Or they want to add to the uniqueness of the place," Spencer said.

"Or they keep prisoners."

Spencer stood up slowly, as though absorbing the information. He walked over to his cluttered dining room table, unearthed an aviation map, and spread it out on the kitchen counter.

"Here's where I air-dropped." He pointed to an area close to Hana. "But this whole thing is—"

"I know," she cut in, meeting his eyes, sensing what he was thinking. "It's a long shot. But I have to try." Looking back to the map, she said, "If you flew me in, how close could I get?"

Spencer stood up straight and a second later the map snapped back into a roll. "You're not doing anything on your own," he said decisively. "You're going to wait for that man to contact you again."

"Just a few hours ago, you wondered if I should even trust the guy."

"And you agreed to wait," he countered.

"Spencer, this is my brother—the only family I have left. Please," she pleaded, rolling the map out once more.

Spencer held her eyes for a moment and then fingered the map again. "The closest I could get would be here."

"How far away is that?"

"About a mile."

Spencer looked up, and Marissa held his gaze squarely. "If I don't hear anything in two more days, will you fly me there?"

A grim line settled around his mouth. "We'll talk about it in two days."

Thirty

Gingerly working his way to a standing position, Michael leaned heavily against the musty concrete wall. Through the bars of his basement cell he saw a deserted campfire that one of the guards had made. The fire was nearly out, but every now and then he would see a small flame leap skyward, struggling to stay alive.

Shivering, he lowered himself back to the dingy mattress. Ugly shadows painted the walls. They were starving him Michael felt his strength . . . his very life slipping away. He lay still, staring up at the rectangular window.

"For the past couple of days, I've been singing this song for you, Issa," he whispered, using the nickname he'd called Marissa when they were kids. Tears ran down his cheek as he tried to make his memory work despite the drugs they continued to force him to take. "What a friend we have in Jesus," he sang hoarsely. "All our sins and griefs to bear; what a privilege to carry everything to God in prayer. Oh, what peace we often forfeit, oh, what needless pain we bear, all because we do not carry everything to God in prayer."

The lyrics seemed to hang in the small cell long after he finished, and he thought of Gabriel. He hadn't shown up for days. Maybe he'd gotten sick and was suffering somewhere. Or maybe they'd discovered his network and he was in a cell of his own.

Any time now, the door would open. He stared, waiting for

the tasteless soup and piece of hardtack. Without Gabriel, there were no sandwiches. The door opened only wide enough for a hand to shove a tray through and then it clicked shut again.

Michael crawled off the dingy mattress. He could feel each rib under his torn, filthy T-shirt. Would the liquid be hot tonight? Sometimes it was and it felt more filling, even satisfying for an hour or so. He felt the bowl. It was warm. Sliding the tray back to the mattress, he wrapped the blanket around him again, cradled the cup in his hands, and closed his eyes. "In this place, this hellish place, I thank you, Jesus, for being here with me. I thank you for what you've taught me. Be with Gabriel . . . protect him and the others held here against their will. As for me," his voice broke and his eyes filled with tears. "God, forgive me for my lack of faith and please, never let me go."

He sipped slowly. The last drops were stone cold. Setting the bowl down, Michael reached for the hardtack. Something felt different. There appeared to be something underneath the stiff piece of paper toweling. Pulling it back, Michael found a slice of bologna with the shape of a cross cut in it. He smiled. Gabriel was still out there.

Thirty-one

*I*f you didn't make all these long-distance calls," Marissa told John, "then who did?"

"It's only twenty-five bucks. Who cares?"

Marissa gave him a cold stare. "That's what you've said about the last ten mysterious bills. The auditors care about stuff like this." Marissa picked up a piece of paper. "Here's a receipt for two flights to Honolulu. It even has your girlfriend's name on it, for Pete's sake." Marissa stuffed the bills into an envelope. "You just can't keep doing this."

"Oh, I get it. You're going to show all those to Spencer and get me fired."

"No," Marissa said, handing him the envelope. "You're going to pay these so you *won't* get fired."

John looked at her for a few seconds and then took the envelope. "If I pay these, you won't say anything?"

"There wouldn't be anything to say, now, would there?"

John eyed her suspiciously. "How about the past stuff?"

"I'm too busy with this quarterly report to research past bills. Of course, if dishonesty rears its ugly head again, I just might find the time."

"Sounds fair." John silently edged to the door, as if not to disturb the good thing that had just happened. "Well, see you tomorrow."

Marissa nodded but didn't look up from the screen. She had

a good four hours worth of work ahead of her.

🍂 🍂 🍂 🍂

"Hey there," Marissa called out when she saw Lynn walk past the office at closing. A moment later Lynn poked her head in the door. "You didn't stop by all evening. Is it really that busy out there or did you find a cute surfer boy to flirt with?" Marissa's smile weakened when Lynn didn't appear amused.

"None of the above," Lynn said.

Marissa decided not to share her latest fiasco with John. Lynn didn't seem in the mood. "How are the kids?"

"You haven't asked me about the kids in weeks. I'm sure you have more important things to do now that you're a suit."

The bell rang. Round one. Well, Marissa didn't want to fight. "I'm sorry if I've been a little preoccupied. You know John's laid practically the whole office responsibility on me."

"You accepted the job."

"I need to pay my bills just like you do," Marissa answered.

"How many children do you have to feed and buy clothes for?"

Marissa swallowed hard. She'd been dragged into the ring, whether she liked it or not. "Look, don't punish me for knowing how to work a computer. That's all it is, you know."

"Right," Lynn said unenthusiastically. "Can I have my paycheck, please?"

"Sure." Marissa picked up a stack of envelopes, flipped through a few, and handed Lynn hers.

Lynn pulled the check out as if to inspect the total, then stuffed it in her purse. "Thanks," she mumbled.

"See you tomorrow," Marissa added.

"Yeah." Lynn paused, as if she wanted to say something more, but she didn't and continued out the door. Marissa heard the restaurant door slide open and then shut again.

Marissa sighed, considering Lynn's distant and hardened words. It would be easy to ignore Lynn and just forget about their friendship, but that wasn't the way to leave things. To-morrow she would get Lynn to talk. It was obvious that something besides work was bothering her.

Marissa was also struck with the idea that there was something different about Lynn. She thought about it for a moment, then shook her head when she couldn't come up with anything specific. She locked the front door, set the alarm, and returned to the office, her deadline paramount.

Twenty minutes later, as she reached for the last of her iced tea, she heard a noise. With her hand hovering over the glass, she listened. Unsure of what she had heard or if she had really heard anything at all, she walked to the office door and peeked out. All was dark and quiet. Still, she decided to investigate. Tip-toeing, she made her way past the pantry entrance. Normally the dimly lit hallway didn't frighten her, but tonight she felt differently. A growing wave of unease swept through her. It wasn't wise to explore on her own. Maybe she should call hotel security.

She paused for a long moment, listening to the hum of the institutional-sized refrigerator as she peered toward the foyer and the double doors beyond. A sound, like a footfall, made her take in a silent, fearful breath. Then a shadow moved in front of the podium. Darting into the kitchen, she pressed up against the stainless-steel counter. Had the intruder seen her? She waited, holding her breath, expecting at any moment for a face to leer at her out of the darkness. But the shadow crossed her narrow view of the hall and crept toward the office.

The day's cash was in the unlocked safe. She should have deposited it in the cash deposit box at closing, but because of the report, she'd put it off. John would most likely berate her, and Spencer would surely be notified. Of course, being robbed was better than being attacked. Slipping off her shoes, she crawled to the opposite side of the doorway where she could see more of the hall. Maybe she could get a glimpse of the perpe-trator—at least provide authorities with a description.

Waiting, she listened for the safe door to squeak as it did every time she or John opened it. But the figure appeared in the doorway only seconds later and slithered toward the break room.

Perplexed at first and then horrified when the matter became clearer, her body trembled. If he wasn't looking for money . . . Her stomach pitched with nausea. She had to get out. Keeping low, she made her way to the door. It was locked. Without keys, she couldn't open the door even from the inside. This person must have gotten in the restaurant with keys and re-locked the door, intentionally trapping her.

She looked over to see the glowing red lights of the alarm system. No lights. The alarm had been unarmed. Suddenly Marissa stiffened as the thing that had been different about Lynn materialized. Her fingernails. Red, expertly manicured fingernails that she usually couldn't afford, especially now, just before payday.

Everyone has a price, Marissa thought grimly. Lynn must have been bought. Her visits to the office could have provided her with the security code John so carelessly posted inside one of the cabinet doors. A sickening feeling wound its way around Marissa's heart. She had considered Lynn fun and honest . . . a friend. Now she was her betrayer.

Sweat trickled down Marissa's temple as she suffered with what to do, where to hide. Tiptoeing deftly, horrified that she might stumble into something that would make a noise, she crept back to the kitchen. She dropped to the floor, and with only a small emergency exit sign for light, she frantically searched for a place to hide. Crawling past a giant free-standing mixer and feeling with her hand along the cabinet front, she searched for the area where the flour and sugar were stored. Finding the cubby hole, she slid in backward under the counter. The darkness felt deadly, and she covered her mouth with the back of her hand as she pressed up against a bag of flour, attempting to conceal her whole body.

Footsteps. The hunter paused at the pantry entrance as if sensing her presence. A beam of light flitted across the room and then began another pass, slower this time. How would it feel to die at the hand of a murderer? Would the pain from the bullet or knife be excruciating, or would it be a quick, sudden death? One more step and the light would expose her foot.

Suddenly bright lights flashed on. She heard footsteps, shouting, and then a scuffle.

"Marissa?" John's voice cried out. "Marissa, are you here?"

Trembling, Marissa crawled out from her hiding place. John was at her side in a matter of seconds. "Are you okay?" he asked, helping her up and then hugging her hard.

Marissa nodded her head stiffly against his shoulder. Squeezing her eyes shut, she took several deep breaths. "How did you know to come?"

"I was in the lobby with—uh, a friend—and saw security guards running to the elevator. They said the alarm had gone off. Sure glad you remembered to set it."

Marissa nodded, half-listening as her eyes panned across the room. An armed guard was handcuffing a woman dressed all in black. She was swearing profusely.

"Is that—" Marissa began, then faltered as she stared at the woman's muscular build and dark hair.

"Yeah," John said, his voice thick with disdain. "She's the scumbag who was trying to rip us off. She's ugly, too."

The woman produced a small, spiteful smile when she saw Marissa look her way. Then she flexed her triceps, making a tattoo undulate on her arm. Marissa stared at the dragon insignia as the woman laughed outright, hysterically.

"Get her out of here," John commanded, putting his arm around Marissa's shoulders, guiding her to the office.

Two policemen arrived minutes later. Marissa answered their questions but didn't offer any additional information, and when they began to cross-examine her, John interrupted. "Don't you think she's been through enough? She told you everything." Then turning to Marissa, John said, "I'll drive you home, okay?"

She nodded dully, still affected by the woman. Strong yet agile, dressed all in black . . . could this woman have been the intruder in Michael's house? The one who took the tapes—possibly evidence?

"I'll put this in here," John was saying as he slipped the cash bag into her tote. "We can drop it in the deposit box on the way out."

Marissa nodded, only half-listening.

As she and John approached the front door, a man with *Action Alarms* emblazoned on his shirt was pulling off the security box cover. "You were one lucky lady," he said, looking over at Marissa. "This thing must have malfunctioned right after you pressed the alarm."

His words seemed to bring Marissa out of her foggy state. "I didn't press the alarm," she said, surprised at the firmness in her voice.

A strange expression crossed the man's face and his eyes grew big as he examined the wires under the cover plate. He turned toward a similarly dressed man and said, "Hey, Gary, come over here. The line's cut and this lady says she never pressed the alarm."

"But it went off," Gary said, eyeing the cut wires in the exposed panel and then looking back to his partner. "I was right there in the control room." Gary turned to Marissa. "Was anyone else here with you?"

"Yes," Marissa said with assurance, the miracle becoming clearer by the minute. "God."

Thirty-two

John drove Marissa home and then insisted on walking through her condo to make sure she was safe. "I know how jumpy you can be after something like this. My sister was mugged over a year ago. She's still a mess."

"I am a little shaky," Marissa admitted, reaching for a bottle of Excedrin in hopes of alleviating the sickening pounding in her forehead.

"I knew a lady who lived in this complex," John said, reappearing from the back bedroom. "She was quite a looker."

Only John could think of a conquest now, Marissa thought, waiting for the rest of his commentary. But as he opened his mouth to proceed, the phone rang, halting any further endorsements by John.

Marissa reached over the sofa to pick up the phone, but John shook his head, indicating she shouldn't answer it. Grabbing the receiver himself, he callously said, "Yeah, who's calling?" playing the protective guardian again. There was a slight pause and his tone softened. "Good. I'll stay here until then.

"Spencer's on his way over," John said, hanging up the phone. "Security called him. He just missed us."

Marissa nodded and sank down on the couch. Numb and slightly chilled, she pulled the quilt from behind her and draped it over her shoulders.

John opened the refrigerator, grabbed two sodas, and

handed her one. Marissa's hands shook as she popped the top. She took a small sip and set it down. Caffeine wasn't what she needed right now.

John turned a dining room chair around and sat in it backward, facing her. "I may not be brilliant," he stated, resting his forearms on the chair back, "but when a robber doesn't go after money in an unlocked safe—" He searched her eyes. "Something's going on with you, isn't it?"

She nodded sagely, staring at the coffee table, reclaiming all the fears she'd given to Jesus that morning.

"Can you fill me in?"

John appeared legitimately concerned and Marissa was touched, but involving one more person wasn't wise. "John, I appreciate you being here for me, but I'd rather not bother you with this."

"I get the message," he said, and when Spencer knocked, John quickly let him in. "One thing I do know. . . ." John picked up his suit jacket and looked back and forth between Marissa and Spencer. "And that's when to leave."

After the door clicked shut behind John, Spencer walked over and gave Marissa a quick hug and then blurted, "You could have been killed." Then he paced the floor, acting as though he didn't know quite what to do.

"Lynn betrayed me," Marissa said softly. "I don't know exactly what she agreed to, but it must have been something." Her voice broke and Spencer sat down next to her. "I thought Lynn was my friend. I can't understand anyone taking money to . . . to . . . harm someone."

When Spencer reached for her hand to comfort her, Marissa found herself shrinking back, a mixture of pain and distrust in her eyes. "How do I know you're not one of them, too? Everyone has a price. What's yours?"

Spencer looked at her incredulously. "You can't honestly believe that I'd betray you?" Spencer sighed as the question hung over the silence that followed.

Marissa struggled with the flood of questions and insecurity that threatened her peace of mind. She wanted to trust him. But she thought Lynn had been a faithful friend, too. *I can't risk another mistake*, she told herself. This one almost cost her life.

"You're just scared." Spencer's words broke into her reverie. "I would be, too. I'm going to help you figure this thing out."

Marissa swallowed hard, trying to steady her voice. "I just need you to fly me to Hana."

"I'm not about to drop you off in the middle of nowhere, Marissa. I care about you." Spencer's voice heightened with emotion. "No, it's more than that. I . . . I love you."

Marissa turned away and bit her lip, holding back tears. "Please don't say things like that. Not now."

"Why not now? We haven't—"

The phone rang, interrupting. They both stared at it for a moment, then Spencer picked up the receiver, meeting Marissa's eyes as he said hello. "Hello," he repeated. He waited a few seconds and then hung up. "The line went dead."

Marissa leaned against the kitchen counter, her head renewing its dull, throbbing pain. They knew too much about her. They were closing in.

"We'll fly at dawn," Spencer suddenly said, standing. "Grab a pair of jeans. Let's get out of here."

Marissa stared at Spencer, stunned by his announcement. But a moment later she hurried to her bedroom and returned armed with an overflowing backpack and her camera. Spencer motioned for her to stay inside as he took a look down the outer staircase. "All clear," he whispered, taking her arm.

"Wait," she said, turning back and grabbing her tote bag. "John and I forgot to deposit the money. Since I may have unwanted guests, I figure it's safer with us."

Spencer nodded impatiently, and together they ran down the stairs.

❧ ❧ ❧ ❧

Sand whipped around them as the helicopter descended

upon the beach. Marissa took off her headset and studied the area, noticing a neglected path that disappeared into the dense jungle a few yards away.

"Looks like we might even have a trail," Marissa observed optimistically.

"Good. It'll save us some time," Spencer replied, his worry glaringly apparent. "Hiking just a short distance through this stuff can take hours." He handed Marissa her backpack and grabbed his own. "And that's all we're doing, remember? Hiking until we see the place, taking some pictures, and leaving."

They'd talked about several plans as they flew. Spencer wasn't happy with any of them that involved a rescue without additional help.

"I can't promise that if I see Michael I'll just take a picture of him and leave," Marissa countered as they walked to the trail. "But don't worry, I won't do anything stupid." She patted the walkie-talkie in her inner chest pocket. "These were a good idea. Thanks."

Twenty yards down the trail, a rat lumbered out of the grass and lifted albino eyes to hers. She gasped, stopping so suddenly that Spencer bumped into her.

"Sorry," she mumbled, running a hand across her brow as the animal crawled away. "I don't like those things." The combination of almost no sleep and raw nerves was making her terribly jumpy.

"We're bound to see more of 'em. Are you sure you don't want me to go first?"

"No, it's okay," Marissa said, determined to keep this crusade her own.

Continuing on, Marissa concentrated on avoiding exposed roots and hanging vines and attempted to keep a steady pace, but a sandstorm of questions whirled in her mind. Would they find Michael? Should she have waited for the man to contact her again? And Spencer. Did he really mean what he said back at the condo—that he loved her? The memory of his words would always remain in her heart, no matter what happened.

A movement in the underbrush caught her eye and suddenly a figure loomed up and lurched onto the trail. Letting out a small cry, Marissa veered away from the outreached hands and Spencer threw out his fist defensively. With a faint groan, the white-suited figure fell to the ground.

Spencer stared, frozen in bewilderment. "I hardly hit him," he softly stated. Spencer looked at Marissa and then nudged the body just in case the man was simply playing the part. He wasn't. Spencer rolled him over. His face was gaunt and one of his too thin legs lay under him at an unnatural angle.

"He's one of them, isn't he?" Marissa said, feelings of anguish washing over her.

"Whoever he is, he needs a doctor," Spencer said, checking his pulse. "Let's splint his leg and fly him to a hospital." Spencer started walking back to the helicopter, but Marissa didn't move. "Come on, we need to get the med kit," he said, walking back and gently taking her hand. "We have proof now. We can call the police."

"No." Marissa's voice was flat, her eyes focused on the skeleton of a man. "I'm not leaving. Michael might be dead by then."

"We'll be back in three or four hours," Spencer pleaded. "With help we'll probably be able to find Michael sooner than we could by ourselves." Still, Marissa wouldn't move. Spencer eyed the surrounding jungle and then looked back at her. "Stay here, then. I'm going to get the med kit."

When Spencer returned with a small canvas suitcase, he looked from the now bare, emaciated body to Marissa. "Why did you take his clothes off?"

"I wanted to check for other injuries," Marissa said, repositioning the balled-up shirt under the unconscious man's head. "It's not like he's nude. He has some sort of sarong on." Marissa didn't meet Spencer's eyes as they worked together building a splint.

"Grab his clothes and the kit, will you?" Spencer said, picking up the inert form. "I'll carry him to the plane."

As Spencer walked away, Marissa's heart pounded hard. She pulled a pen from her pocket, ripped off an airline ID tag hanging from Spencer's pack, and scratched a note. Spencer wouldn't want her to continue on alone, but Michael could be feigning survival just like this man. She had to get to him. Securing the note on top of Spencer's pack with a clump of red dirt, she snatched up the man's clothes and bolted deeper into the jungle.

Thirty-three

Running the narrow path as fast as she could, Marissa prayed Spencer wouldn't follow. He needed to help the dying man and contact the police. She needed to find Michael.

When the trail veered inland near a trickling waterfall, she slowed to navigate across patches of slippery rocks. A few feet later the foliage thickened, making it hard to discriminate the trail. Several times Marissa contemplated hiking back to the waterfall and following the beach, but she feared becoming disoriented and getting completely lost.

Pausing after an hour's walk, she wiped the sweat from her forehead, frustrated by her situation. Maybe it had been foolish to act on impulse and go off by herself. No doubt Spencer had flown back with the man. She prayed he was getting help.

The trail had eroded to almost nothing when she chose to walk through the knee-high grass toward what looked to be a less dense area two yards ahead. She walked cautiously, hoping no rats were underfoot and thankful that the island didn't host snakes. As she proceeded, her foot struck a stone. She looked down and saw a weather-worn tombstone. She pushed the grass away to her left and then her right. Tombstones were all around her. She was in the middle of an ancient burial site. As she took a step backward, her foot sunk in some freshly turned dirt. Her heart pounded hard. She turned around and saw a rectangular pattern on the ground. A recently dug grave.

Panic seized her and she quickly weaved her way through the stones and away from any atrocities that may lay claim to the graves. Barely slowing to forge a shallow ravine, she scrambled up a small hill, then stopped short when she saw something move. She darted under a blanket of monstera leaves and waited, listening. Finally, she parted the leaves and saw a white-clad figure walking away toward a clearing. Had her wild dash led her to the resort? Marissa searched the area with her eyes for a long moment, and then, stealthily, she made her way closer.

Crouched behind a veil of ferns, she saw a gray-and-white stucco building in the middle of a grassy area that turned to sand near the beach. People wandered the grounds, talking, laughing, appearing healthy—not at all like the scene she had imagined. A canopy extended from the building with long rows of picnic tables underneath, and the figure who had walked from the jungle was a woman who was now busily arranging a bouquet of wild flowers in a vase. Maybe her hunch was wrong about the cult being there.

Her eyes slowly passed over the drab rise of the structure again, then flew back in alert curiosity. Basement windows with bars on them. She pulled out her camera and zoomed in on the opening, but she couldn't see anything past the bars. Crawling under the fern cover, trying to get a closer look, she noticed a group of white-clad subjects sitting silent and staring at a large lava rock. Anxiously, she looked for Michael, but no figure was tall enough.

After capturing all she could on film, she exchanged the camera for the walkie-talkie—nothing but static. Spencer had most likely brought the sick man to Kahului and was too far away to contact. She looked back to the circle of people. They were standing now, chanting something together over and over as the leader led them toward a jungle path.

Marissa's heart thundered as she removed her backpack and slipped the boat-necked shirt on over her head, trying to ignore the stench left from the previous owner. She pulled on the elastic-waisted pants and then crouched, waiting. *Do I have the cour-*

age to do this? she questioned, then reminded herself that Spencer knew where she was. He was certainly bringing help. She couldn't just ignore this opportunity.

Emerging from the underbrush, Marissa caught up with the cluster, hoping their transcendental session would dull their memory of who was in the group. She followed the last person in line, adapting to her pace. As if sensing someone behind her, the woman turned. Marissa stared wide-eyed at Renae.

"Marissa!" Renae said excitedly. "I didn't know you were coming to this. How long have you been here?"

"I just got here . . . today. How about you?" Marissa's hands felt clammy and she nervously smoothed her hair, wondering how disheveled she looked. She didn't know if seeing Renae was good or bad.

"It's my last day," Renae said as she moved over on the path so they could walk side by side. "I've been here a week. You're going to love it. The morning yoga is great, the food is delicious, and oh, they have the best crystal selection I've ever seen. You really get the chance to clear your mind here. Everything is so down-to-earth." Suddenly Marissa realized that this was the resort one could go to at the end of the "Power for Success" class.

"Is that why you came," Marissa asked, "for the natural lifestyle?"

Renae nodded, taking in a deep breath. "It's been wonderful getting away from an artificial environment. I've been listening to the birds and quieting my mind. It's been a spiritual rebirth, especially the chakra balancing. I feel like I'm connecting with the real me."

"Interesting," Marissa replied, forcing a smile. "How's work? Did you get that promotion you were putting in all those hours for?"

"No," Renae said with surprising goodheartedness. "I've learned that having material things isn't that important. I want to try to live simpler. I even sold my house this week."

"Here?"

"Yeah. It was providence. Steve knew of this guy who

wanted it, and I've already invested half the money in resorts like this. Being an investor, I get a fifty percent discount, and they plan to open resorts worldwide. I'm happy and I feel so free—that's all that really matters, you know."

"Well, good for you," Marissa concluded, managing a smile despite her frustration over hearing what sounded like a scam under the guise of spiritual rebirth.

"They may even make a training center out of my house," Renae continued, "although Steve said they're mainly looking for places on the West Coast."

Marissa took in a ragged breath. Her parent's estate in Portland was like this—large, surrounded by trees, away from a main highway—it could be another site for them. A place where attendees could be swayed under the guise of devas, guides, and imagery. Silent rage filled her.

"After this nature walk, we're having lunch," Renae said. "Want to sit together?"

Marissa nodded weakly.

Once inside the building, Marissa dabbed at the sweat on her face with the back of her hand and then motioned toward a door marked *Women*. "This heat has gotten to me," she told Renae. "I think I'll freshen up before lunch."

"Okay, but then come find me," Renae said. "I usually sit at the tables near the beach." Marissa nodded and Renae continued with the others.

Marissa latched the flimsy lock on the toilet stall door and pressed her back against the cool tile wall. What apostasies and evil were nurtured in this place? What lies perpetuated? Her mouth tasted acrid and she stifled the impulse to run out of the building and back to the jungle . . . far away from there.

" 'Let the morning bring me word of your unfailing love,' " she whispered, repeating a Bible verse Myrtle had given her weeks ago, " 'for I have put my trust in you. Show me the way

I should go, for to you I lift up my soul.' " God's Word renewed her. She clung to the security.

Exiting the bathroom, she continued down the hall until she found steps leading down. Was Michael down there? Warily, she followed the steps to a dimly lit hallway. Several doors were on either side. Hands trembling, she opened the first door. A furnace room. She tiptoed to the next. Locked. The third door was locked, too. Suddenly, out of nowhere, a hand grabbed her and pushed her up against the wall. "What are you doing down here?" a heavyset, bearded man demanded.

"I'm—I'm lost," she said, her voice wobbling horribly. "I was trying to find the cafeteria."

"The cafeteria?" the man said mockingly. "Where's your room key?"

Marissa swallowed hard and a trickle of sweat rolled down her back. "I forgot it."

"We don't lock our doors here," the man snarled with a glare as his grip on her shoulder tightened. With his free hand, he pulled a knife from his pocket. Half smiling, he moved the blade to her throat, seeming to enjoy the torture he inflicted. He then brought the knife to her chest, pierced the material, and dragged the blade down, cutting open the tunic. Immediately, he noticed her belt pack. "Open it," he demanded, motioning to the pack. With the knife again against her throat, she did as he asked.

When he saw the walkie-talkie and camera, he assaulted her with a tirade of curses, pulled her by her hair, and locked her in a room that was bare except for a light bulb hanging from the ceiling. Terrified, she huddled in a corner. *Stupid*, Marissa thought to herself. *I don't qualify as courageous—just stupid.* Now she was trapped just like Michael.

Minutes later the door burst open and two men appeared. The shorter, blond-haired man walked over and glared down at Marissa.

"What's your name?" he demanded.

When she didn't answer, the thicker man approached and

backhanded her in the face. She flinched at the pain and tasted blood.

"Let's try again," the blonde said, his voice controlled. "What's your name?"

She took a sharp breath when Mr. Thick pulled his arm back for a second blow. "Marissa Tomsen," she blurted.

The blond man looked at her for a moment and then produced a low chuckle. "You've saved us a lot of trouble by coming here yourself."

"Where's Michael?" she said, looking him straight in the eye.

"Don't worry about him. Worry about yourself. He's ours."

"No, he isn't." She wiped blood from her lip. "He'd never fall for your lies."

The blonde gave her a cold glare, motioned to the bone-crusher, and walked out of the room. The second slap to her face was brutal and Marissa cried out in pain. The next blow rendered her unconscious.

આ&ab;   આ&ab;   આ&ab;   આ&ab;

"Marissa?" A voice floated above her, or was it beside her? Something touched her cheek, a hand weaker than hers—cold and shaky. She opened her eyes and saw a blurred face that slowly came into focus.

"Michael?" she said, struggling to get up. Propped against the wall, Michael was barely able to sit, much less walk. His unshaven face was haggard and nearly unrecognizable. "Oh, Michael," she repeated, pulling his gaunt frame close. "What have they done to you?"

Tears rolled down Michael's face. "You shouldn't have come," he said, taking a labored breath. "You don't deserve suffering for my mistakes."

"You don't deserve this, either," Marissa said, already repulsed by the hideous smells and dirty surroundings. She smiled, despite her bruised face and cracked lip. "I found your note and necklace," she said, squeezing his hand. "I'm so glad you remembered the code. Did you ever guess as kids that we'd—"

"End up dying here?" Michael finished.

Marissa swallowed hard as reality screamed, deafening. Finding Michael had been her sole purpose for so long, but now that she had found him she felt utterly useless. This wasn't the victory she had envisioned. She had taken a step beyond her own fear in coming there. Still, she refused to give in to it. "We're not going to die here," she said firmly. "We're getting out."

"How?"

"A man named Spencer is getting help right now." Marissa pushed back an oily strand of Michael's hair. "He has a helicopter and he knows where we are."

Michael took a labored breath and his eyes flickered shut as he rested his head against her shoulder. "Does Gabriel know you're here?"

"Who's Gabriel?"

He smiled slightly "You know, the angel."

Thirty-four

Two hours later the door to the small cell flung open.

"A family reunion. How tender." Even in the dim light, Marissa recognized the voice. "Persistence got you here," Steve said, walking in, "but it won't get you out." His entourage, a bodyguard and an old man, stood silent behind him.

"I know about the will money and your plans for the estate," Marissa said, putting a protective hand on Michael.

"A little Nancy Drew, are you?"

"You can have the money and the house on the condition you let us go."

He laughed with the same smug self-confidence she had grown to despise. "I don't need conditions."

"If my brother stays here any longer, he'll die—and you'll be up for murder."

"Murder?" Steve laughed. "How about suicide? Michael is a drug addict. Once we get him back to Portland, he won't live long and his autopsy will prove an overdose. Don't worry," Steve said with a slow smile as he nodded to the old man. "He's not feeling much of this."

The old man carried over a small paper cup filled with a red liquid and knelt near Michael's mattress. At first Marissa didn't understand, but when the man lifted Michael's head so he could drink, she cried out, "No!" and lunged to intercede. She wouldn't let them give him any more drugs—not in front of her, not without a fight. Ready for her response, the bodyguard pulled her back and held her hard against him, breathing foul air in her face.

After the drug was administered, Marissa twisted loose and scrambled across the floor. Using the hem of her shirt, she wiped frantically at Michael's mouth. If she could save him from one drop of the poison, she would.

"We'll begin your treatment tomorrow," Steve said. Then walking to the door, he added, "Too bad drug addiction runs in your family."

Marissa continued wiping the sticky liquid from Michael's mouth, not giving him the satisfaction of knowing how deep his words cut. What kind of person could do this to another? Would Michael die in a few hours? A feeling of hopelessness weighed heavy on her shoulders.

The old man was still down on his knees. She felt him looking at her, but she ignored him and only hoped he would leave. She didn't need another evil face to haunt her. But then she heard him whisper something—words she thought she'd never hear in that awful place. "God is faithful."

Her eyes flew to his. The man's face was turned away from the guard, but she could see him clearly—kind eyes that spoke of love and concern. Could she dare hope upon hope, or was her desire to find an alliance so powerful she had made one up? As the man stood, the prosaic look returned to his eyes, and he followed the guard out.

"Michael," Marissa whispered, bending low to the mattress. "Can you hear me? Please stay alive."

Michael tried to open his eyes for Marissa, but the drug overcame him. His eyes rolled back as he fell into unconsciousness.

Marissa cried as she stroked Michael's cheek, and a great sadness draped over her. *Was* God faithful? Hadn't she struggled and risked everything to help Michael? What more could she do? Lonely and scared, she watched the shadows fade, throwing the cell into darkness.

ॐ ॐ ॐ ॐ

Marissa woke up hours later, shivery cold on the foot of the mattress. The sound of a key turning in the lock made her hopeful for food and she sat up, rubbing her arms, trying to get warm. Michael was still asleep, but his chest rose and fell regularly and she had covered him with the blanket so she hoped he was warm. The door opened and the guard appeared with the old man, who was carrying another small cup.

"No, please, no," she pleaded, realizing exactly what was going to happen. But again, the guard held her firmly as the old man made Michael drink the drug. Afterward the guard pushed her aside and then barked at the old man, "Where's hers?"

"I'll get it," the old man mumbled.

Tears rolled a silent path down Marissa's face as she knelt near her brother and wiped his mouth. Is this how she would end up, too? She wanted to get married one day, have a baby. Being healthy and physically fit was always a gift she was thankful for. Now would she waste away to Michael's state? *Why, God?*

When the old man returned, the guard pulled her to her feet saying, "If you spill any, you'll lick it up off the floor."

Hesitantly, she turned toward the old man. He held out the cup to her but at the same time pressed a piece of paper into her hand. Concealing the paper and clinging to the kindness in his eyes, she drank the liquid. No bitterness. A moment later they were gone and a key turned in the lock. Waiting until the footsteps faded, Marissa unfolded the small piece of paper with trembling fingers. *When the whistle blows, climb out, head for the dock. A boat will be there.*

Climb out? Escape? There were bars across the only opening in the room, and guards routinely patrolled the hallway. She could hear them. How could this man promise anything when he seemed as much a prisoner as they were? And if Michael was as groggy as last night, he wouldn't be able to walk anywhere. Was this just part of a sick game Steve was playing?

As she ripped the note up and stuffed it into her jeans

pocket, she heard Michael whisper, "Hey, Issa." She turned around to see his eyelids fluttering open. "Want some food?" he asked. He moved back a corner of his blanket and there sat a small but thick sandwich.

"How did you get that?" Marissa asked, surprise on her face.

"The old man," Michael said.

"He's your friend?" Marissa said, hope renewing in her heart.

"He's my angel," Michael whispered, his eyes closing again. "Name's Gabriel. He gave me medicine tonight. I'll be stronger when I wake up later."

Marissa stared in silent amazement, fitting things together. No wonder Michael called Gabriel his angel—apparently the old man had been keeping Michael alive. She wanted to ask Michael more, but the medicine affected him and he seemed to be sleeping—comfortably this time.

Will it only be a few minutes, or will it be countless hours before the whistle blows? she wondered. The old man surely wouldn't wait long. He knew how sick Michael was. She walked to the window envisioning Spencer's helicopter landing on the beach directly in front of her, Spencer running to the window, cutting the bars, and all three of them leaving in the chopper, safe. But it was only a dream.

Michael had no doubt spent hours dreaming and looking out this window, watching the ocean reach its foamy fingers toward the sand, inching its way farther and farther up the beach and then back again. She gripped the bars, her stomach growling despite half the sandwich she'd eaten. Being here would either make you hate everyone, including God, or bring you closer—closer than you'd ever been. Marissa wondered how Michael had reacted to their brainwashing techniques. Had their slow twist of the truth taken away his faith in Jesus?

Wearily she let go of the bars. Then she turned back. Something felt strange. She touched the bars again—a slight movement. She worked them up and down and then pushed. To her amazement, they opened outward.

Excitement pulsed through her as the chance of escape danced across her soul. Stretching her arm out, she clutched a handful of sand and joyfully let the tiny particles sift through her fingers. The same sand she'd complained about being in every pair of her shoes brought renewed energy.

"Thank you, God," she whispered. They could climb out, just as Gabriel instructed. She would find the dock, and the waiting boat would take them away from this detestable place. Setting the bars back in place, she buttoned Michael's shirt, put on his shoes, and waited for the whistle to sound.

Thirty-five

*J*ours crept by. Darkness settled in. Marissa paced the small cell. Had something happened to Gabriel? Or had he given the signal and she hadn't heard? Now appeared to be the perfect time to escape, with low clouds making visibility on the water poor.

Another hour. Michael awoke, and Marissa helped him sit up by leaning him against the wall. "Here's some soup," she said, helping him with the bowl that had been slid inside the room hours ago.

"This is cold," he said, soup dripping off his chin. "Don't give the waiter a tip tonight, okay?" He half smiled but still looked incredibly weak and gaunt, and his attempt at humor only made her remember happier times.

She handed him the remaining half of the sandwich Gabriel had given them and tried to return the smile.

"What's with the shoes?" he said, looking down at his feet.

"We're escaping," she whispered.

"We are? When?"

Marissa was so anxious that she could barely think. She looked out the window again and then back to Michael.

If she jumped the whistle, so be it. She'd rather wait on the beach than here. "Now," she said, standing. She set the empty bowl near the door, listened for a moment, then walked to the window, pushing the bars outward and propping them up with one of her shoes.

A spark came to Michael's eyes as Marissa helped him to the window. "Gabriel?" he whispered, hope brightening his face.

Marissa nodded.

"He said he was going to get me out. Told me to have patience."

Marissa paused, reconsidering her decision to leave. Maybe they should wait. But freedom was right through the window. She'd touched the sand, felt the warm breeze on her face.

"I'll go first and check things out," she whispered.

Marissa pulled herself up a few inches, gripped the cement sides, and crawled out. Continuing on her stomach past a cluster of young palm trees, she waited, silent and still. Slowly, she inched her way five more feet until she cleared the foliage and saw the outline of a dock off to the right. There was no boat, but they would be ready when it arrived.

"I see the dock," she whispered to Michael after she'd crawled back. "It's not far."

Michael's expression faltered, as if remembering the last time he'd made it to the dock. Marissa watched as a look of trust and determination replaced his apprehension. He appeared ready to try—with her support.

With a great deal of help from Marissa, and favoring his injured leg, Michael maneuvered his way out. He was sweating profusely when they lay side by side near the palm trees. Though he never complained, Marissa could hear the quiet pleas for God's help Michael said under his breath. It was obvious that his gangrenous leg was causing him intense pain.

"Let's crawl," Marissa whispered.

Michael nodded, gritted his teeth, and began the painstaking process of pulling himself forward inch by inch. He moved incomprehensibly slow. "You go ahead," he said, sensing Marissa's anxiousness.

"No," Marissa said, her voice firm. "Let's try walking. You can lean on me."

Fueled more so by fear than energy, she helped him up, put his right arm across her shoulder, and supported him around the waist. Just two days without food had claimed much of her strength. She couldn't imagine Michael's struggle.

At first he leaned lightly against her, walking mostly on his own power. But the farther they went, the more he inclined until she was practically dragging him. Exhausted, she finally let him sink to the sand. "We'll rest here," she said, breathing hard.

Marissa's eyes traveled the horizon. Off to the right there was a pile of driftwood and beyond that a rocky beach. To the left was a sandy beach that curved out of sight. Twenty yards straight ahead was the dock. They could wait for the boat in shoulder-high water behind the pilings. She looked back toward the building. Everything looked copacetic. Still, she was anxious to reach the dock.

Just as she was about to nudge Michael, a whining sound made her take another look back to the left. Dune buggies, three in staggered positions, were headed straight for them. Marissa froze, staring at the headlights bobbing up and down. Guards patrolling the beach? Or had someone already discovered Michael's empty cell?

Scrambling to her knees, Marissa shook Michael's still form. "Michael. Someone's coming. We have to move."

Michael attempted to get up, but he collapsed a moment later, submitting to dizziness and exhaustion. "You go," he said feebly. "Leave me."

"I didn't come here to give up." Marissa's pronouncement was as much for herself as for Michael. Marissa looked toward the headlights again and then back to Michael. Rolling him on his back, she stooped in front of him, grasped his hands, and pulled. "Hide us, God," she whispered.

In four tenuous pulls, she reached the wood and rolled Michael next to the largest piece. Lying close beside, she peered through a knothole and watched the bobbing lights grow larger, brighter.

"I don't think they saw us," she said. Michael had curled up into a ball with his eyes closed. She wanted to say something to encourage him. Instead she found herself looking back toward the oncoming machines as the whining grew louder. She could hear the drivers yelling at one another now, cursing and egging one another on.

Antenna waving violently in the air, the first machine crossed dangerously close in front of the second and then raced ahead. A moment later the second machine followed in pursuit. The third driver swerved to avoid the sand and spray produced by the others and accelerated straight for the driftwood. Marissa clutched Michael's shoulder. He was going to crash into them! Shielding both their heads, Marissa braced herself.

The buggy hit hard and a body vaulted over their heads. Seconds later the machine died. Jolted but uninjured, Marissa checked Michael and then cautiously peered over the wood. The driver lay face first on the sand. His machine was tipped on its side but still in one piece.

Marissa waited for the figure to move. It didn't. She could hear the high-pitched motors of the other two machines continuing in the other direction—the drivers apparently unaware of the mishap. She eyed the dune buggy. They had to take this opportunity. The others would certainly be back soon, and then she and Michael would be discovered for sure.

Marissa picked up a stick and held it, poised and ready, as she crawled past the prone man. Evaluating the buggy, she determined it was still driveable. But they would have to move quickly, for the driver could come to any moment.

"We have a ride," Marissa whispered, helping Michael up. She half carried, half dragged him to the dune buggy—clumsily helping him climb under the rollbar and into the bucket seat. Then she squeezed in herself.

She glanced toward the dock—still no boat. She looked the direction the other two buggies had gone. The sound of their machines had grown faint. Maybe she and Michael had a chance.

"Hold on," she told Michael, turning over the engine and squeezing the handle. Unprepared for the initial jolt, Marissa temporarily lost her grip, but a second later, she grasped the bar tighter and they shot out toward the hard-packed sand close to the ocean. She glanced over at Michael. He looked disoriented. She had to get as far away as possible before the drivers came back looking for their friend. Marissa squeezed the handlebar tight, hitting top speed. If only they could find a house, a cabin, a boat—anything.

The droplets of water felt refreshing on her face, and every foot that distanced them from the resort helped replenish her confidence. But several turns later, the beach became narrow, and farther up, cliffs created an uncontested dead end.

Marissa slowed the dune buggy and headed for the jungle. For five precious minutes she searched for a path, but it was useless in the dark. Finally, she plowed in at one of the less dense areas, and as she expected, they only gained a few yards through the thick vegetation before the engine choked. Marissa knew they had to move on, though, for daylight would reveal the tire tracks.

"We have to get away from this machine," Marissa said, helping Michael out.

"The boat?" Michael's voice was weak.

Marissa's heart ached. Her impatience had cost them dearly—maybe even their lives. "Not yet," she said, supporting him. "Can you walk a little?" He tried, but the ground was uneven, and when there was nowhere to go but up a steep incline, he collapsed.

Marissa squeezed her eyes shut and held him tight. She didn't want to leave him, but there was no other way. If she found help quickly, she could rescue Michael before they found him. Crying softly, she pulled him under a thick grove of ferns and made him as comfortable as possible.

"I'll be back," she said, wiping her eyes and then kissing him on the cheek. "I promise." She covered him with more ferns, oriented herself with where she would come back for him, and scrambled up the steep slope.

Marissa frantically hiked inland, running the easier terrain and all the while trying to remember where the nearest road was on Spencer's map. Her only stops were for a quick drink from a small waterfall and to grab a low-hanging mango that she ate as she walked. Still, she felt guilty about eating and drinking, knowing Michael could do neither.

Exhausted, but stimulated by the challenge before her, she reached the road at dawn. Unwilling to wave down any vehicle coming from the north, in case it would be one from the resort, she hid behind a cluster of ferns and held out for a car going the opposite direction.

Finally, one came. Emerging from the ferns, Marissa waved eagerly. The car stopped. It was probably too early to be a tourist, but hopefully a willing native could be of help. The driver's door opened, and Marissa sucked in her breath. It was Steve. A second later a guard jumped out.

Darting back into the bushes, she ran until a pair of heavier footsteps overtook her, and strong arms dragged her toward the road.

"I have to get my brother," she told the guard, fighting tears of frustration.

"We have your dear brother," Steve called to her. "And if you don't hurry, he'll die here instead of his place in Portland. That wouldn't make me happy." After being shoved roughly against the car, she climbed in the backseat. There was Michael, gaunt and stooped. Putting her arms around him, she cried out to God for mercy.

An hour later Marissa sat in a tiny hut, her ankles and wrists bound. Michael lay beside her. She could hear a muted conversation between Steve and two other men on the other side of a bamboo divider.

"Get Mike to Portland on the company jet," Steve was saying. "We don't need any more blood on our hands. You'll have to do the woman here. She knows too much. Make it an accident, whatever. I'm going back to base. I'll send someone out to pick you up." Two doors slammed and a car drove away.

Trembling over her impending death, Marissa wondered what sense all this made for God's kingdom. Why was God allowing this to happen? Hadn't she done the right thing by not giving up on Michael?

A group of voices heightened outside her bamboo cell, and she inched her way over to a crack in the wall so she could see. *Spencer!* Her heart leaped with elation. Seeing his familiar face immediately brought a sense of comfort and security. But her joy was short-lived when she realized that if Spencer wasn't with the police, he, too, must have been captured. She had jeopardized his life, as well. Grief took an even more strangling grip on her senses. Now there were three of them living the same nightmare. She stared at him through the crack, agonizing.

But then Marissa noticed something strange. Spencer wasn't bound like she was. He had his pack looped around one shoulder and appeared unscathed, looking comfortable standing next to the other men.

"He's a pilot," the accompanying guard said to the other two. "Said he'd fly us to Honolulu." Then he chuckled. "The girl wasn't too smart. She paid him in advance."

Stunned and confused, Marissa looked toward Spencer. His back was to her, but she could hear his laughter mingling with theirs. Then she caught sight of what Spencer was holding—the restaurant's safe deposit bag. He'd betrayed her—lied! How could he? Or had he been one of them all along?

Thirty-six

*S*till reeling from Spencer's deception, Marissa pulled her eyes away only when someone was pushed inside the small hut. "You don't have to do it this way, Cecil," Hiram was saying.

"Just get in the back with the others," the Samoan man said, giving Hiram another shove.

"Cecil, can't you just—"

"You know the plans," Cecil interrupted, his stony complexion as dark as his mood.

When Hiram stumbled into the room, he took a quick glance at Marissa, then sank to his knees beside Michael. "This boy—" Hiram paused, his eyes assessing Michael. "He needs a doctor."

"No, he doesn't. But in a few hours he'll need a funeral. You all will."

Hiram looked ill. "I can make this legal without—"

"Save your breath." Cecil handcuffed Hiram to an iron handle on the floor. "Steve said you weren't the best accountant anyway." He threw Hiram's attaché on the floor and left.

Hiram sat staring at Michael with his shoulders hunched, looking twice his age. Marissa looked away. How different Hiram was from her mother. Prayer would have been her stance, brokeness was his. Hiram had no one. Not even God.

"I didn't know this would happen," Hiram finally said, his

voice despondent and low. "I never knew that—" His voice cracked and he started to cry.

When I am weak, then I am strong, Marissa thought, remembering another Bible verse. Even in this wretched situation, God was there, the Author of all hope, the Creator, her personal friend.

"Hiram." Marissa's tone was soft, but he only wiped his nose and didn't look up. "Mom never stopped praying for you. I think it's time you prayed for yourself."

Hiram shook his head miserably. "No . . . there's no hope for me."

"There is," Marissa urged, her voice stronger, more confident. "Forget the past. God will."

Hiram lifted despairing eyes, as if considering her words. But the door opened and Cecil came storming in. "We're leaving," he announced, untying the ropes around Marissa's ankles and unlocking Hiram's handcuffs. "Help me out with him," he said to Hiram, motioning to Michael.

Marissa stood stiffly and followed them out to where two men sat smoking beside a small campfire. The smell of marijuana was strong in the air. Hiram propped Michael up under a mango tree, then fumbled trying to keep him from falling over, acting as though caring for someone was awkward and something he'd rarely done.

"The broad needs to have a little accident," Cecil announced. "Tai," he said, looking toward a pock-faced young man whose eyes were partially covered by oily strands of coal-black hair. "You do it. It'll be good experience for you."

Tai took one last drag of his handmade cigarette, threw the remains into the campfire, and stood. "The cliff?" he asked.

Cecil nodded. "If she doesn't die from the fall, she'll drown in the water. Then Uncle won't feel so responsible, will you?" Cecil gave Hiram an evil smile.

Hiram only stared at the fire, as if in a trance.

"He didn't say no, so I guess he agrees," Cecil taunted. "Just make sure she's dead. Because if she isn't—" he paused, giving his words mastery—"you'll be. Understand?"

Tai was younger, but his eyes were hardened like the others. Perhaps even more so because of his age. Pulling a knife from his pocket, he cut the ropes around Marissa's wrists with two savage slashes. "Get up," he commanded.

"Wait," Marissa said, crawling over to Michael. "I have to say good-bye." Michael appeared unconscious, but the moment Marissa's arms encircled him, his eyes fluttered open and he smiled weakly.

"Home?" he murmured. Tears streamed down Marissa's face. She was scared to die, scared to lose her brother. The world seemed terribly dark.

"I love you, Michael," she whispered. "God loves you, too."

His breath was faint, but she could hear his belabored words. "Jesus loves me, this I know." The words to the familiar children's song were poignant—revealing to Marissa that Michael still felt Jesus' love, despite what they had done to him.

"Get up," Tai barked, grabbing her hair and jerking her backward. Michael's gaunt frame fell forward with Marissa, and when Tai dragged her to her feet, he lay face first in the dirt.

"Pick him up," she screamed to Hiram. "Pick him up." But Hiram remained motionless, staring into the fire.

Suddenly Spencer appeared from a trail behind them, ran over, and gently eased Michael onto his back. Seeing Spencer evoked a myriad of emotions, the strongest being anger at his traitorous ways.

"How can you let them do this to me?" Marissa's cry resounded through the shroud of silence. She wanted Spencer to turn around so he could witness firsthand the terror in her eyes. "How can you let them kill me?" She spat out the words, not understanding anything, letting the surrounding evil cloud her thoughts.

Spencer turned, and for an instant she saw love, compassion, and deep pain in his eyes. But a second later they turned cool.

"You lost the bet, remember," Spencer said. "Denver 3, Vikings 2."

"Now that's cold." Cecil laughed. "Are you going to go through her pockets for the money, too?"

"Come on." Tai, terse with responsibility, shoved her forward. Marissa stumbled, but then regained her balance and straightened her shoulders. She would leave Spencer and the others with dignity. Let this memory be their shame.

Still, fear wrapped around her senses like an evil cocoon, and as they began the ascent, her breathing became short and erratic. She felt the first throes of nausea. There was a ringing in her ears; she couldn't hear, couldn't think. She just walked, with Tai directly behind her.

God, let it be quick, she started praying, but instead of persistent thoughts of death, Spencer's words replayed in her head. *Denver 3, Vikings 2. Denver 3, Vikings 2.* Why had he said such a thing? A sudden revelation nearly caused her to halt her steps. *Could it be?* Forcing her mind to think in code, she spelled out D-I-V-E. *Dive.* Dive where? Off the cliff she was to be thrown?

When she caught a glimpse of a row of rotten trees up the path, her steps slowed. Could these be the same trees she noticed during her climb down to the cave? As a journalist, Michael often told her that information was powerful, but what advantage was there in knowing how steep the cliff was, or that she would break her neck in the water below? Unless . . .

Suddenly a fist slammed into her shoulder, throwing her hard to the ground. Tai glared, towering over her. "I'll kill you with my bare hands if you don't move faster."

Terror renewed its savage threat as she realized the intensity of her slayer. A successful murder would no doubt prove to the rest that he had the right stuff. She had only one chance—if that.

She stood, already feeling tenderness in her shoulder. Ten more feet. She eyed the jungle as fear welled up in her throat. *God, help me*, she silently cried. Leaping forward and then darting to the cliff side, Marissa plunged into the dense foliage. After two steps, the ground disappeared under her and she slid vertically fifteen feet. Branches skinned and slapped her face and arms with welting sharpness. Grabbing at vines and branches, she slowed enough to control the fall. Tai was close behind, cursing and gaining on her.

When her foot caught on a root, Tai grabbed a handful of her hair and snapped her head back. Crying out in pain, her hands clawed at his. Suddenly the rocks began sliding. Tai lost his grip and caught a tree branch. Marissa screamed as she continued sliding, desperate to stop before she reached sheer rock. With bloody hands, she clutched at root after root until one held. With her feet dangling and her face pressed to the rock wall, she hung precariously. Frantic for a foothold, her toes found a small but secure rock. She took a few shuddering breaths and then looked up. Tai was a yard above her, holding on with one arm and struggling to pull a gun from his pocket with the other. There was only one way to escape and no time to consider the risks. Pivoting to her right, she dived.

Thirty-seven

Marissa was in the air forever, falling an eternity. Faces, memories flashed before her eyes. Was it she who was screaming or someone else? Cold water enveloped her face, pouring into her nostrils, her ears, and forcing its way down her throat. Even with her back strained and fully arched, she submerged deeper and deeper. She wasn't going to make it. The water was too shallow. She sensed the terrible force with which she would crash into the rocky bottom.

Seconds later she felt a different sensation. Was she really traveling upward, or had she already died and God was taking her to heaven? Her hands broke the surface and then struck against something hard. Her head hit the same object, but with less force. Dunked under, she quickly resurfaced and gulped in air, gasp after gasp, unable to fully comprehend the miracle that had just happened.

"Thank you, God. Oh, thank you," she whispered in uneven phrases as she clung to the cavernous rock wall in the back corner of the pool. The dive flashed through her mind in riveting clarity, over and over. It had been a miracle—a blessed miracle.

In the dimness, with water only inches from the ceiling, she maneuvered around until she saw a slit of sunlight near the rock opening. Cautiously, she edged over. Her killer. Was he still out there waiting for her to surface? Hidden in the shade, still breathing unevenly, she surveyed the cliff. There. Her eyes fixed on a movement in the trees. He was climbing back up, making his way over and down to the plateau Spencer had dived from. Did he assume she was still alive? Or maybe he just wanted to see her floating corpse.

Trembling, she watched Tai shade his eyes and peer down, looking at the water. He paced the small area nervously. His life was on the line and he appeared extremely agitated. He looked down at the pool again and then back toward camp. Suddenly he jerked off his T-shirt and began climbing down.

Marissa gasped. He was going to search the pool.

Pulling herself toward the back wall, she felt she had no energy left to think, much less do anything physical. But she had to. She had to find the cave.

Everything looked different from how it had been when she was with Spencer. The water was higher and hid the large rock she remembered clinging to just before Spencer took her under. Using her feet, she searched for the underwater rock while furtive glances back toward the opening caused her to envision Tai's silhouette looming up any second. Or he might be approaching underwater, reaching to pull her under.

Tears of frustration slipped down her face and into the water as her search became more frantic. Finally, she felt the rock and a different kind of fear possessed her. "Jesus, lead me through," she whispered, terrified of the underwater swim, but even more of her predator.

Holding her third deep breath, she pulled herself down, felt along the wall until her hands touched nothing, and then pushed her way into the black hole. Kicking strong and hard, she propelled herself forward until her lungs felt as if they would burst. Then she paddled straight up. She had either entered the cave or her watery grave.

Her head broke through the water into open space and she greedily took in great gulps of air. Arms and legs moving in jerky patterns, she managed to keep her head above the surface. The ledge was only a few inches away. She felt something brush her leg, and with panicked movements, she heaved herself up and away from any creatures, real or imagined, lurking below. Fatigue and shock caused her to tremble, and she crawled to the farthest corner and huddled with her knees drawn up tight. She stared at the dark entrance, praying her killer knew nothing of this cave.

ॐ ॐ ॐ ॐ

Hours later and shivering violently, Marissa heard a noise. Holding her cramped legs, she listened. It was a voice—a man's voice. One? Two? She didn't know. Was it Tai, or some of the others?

Swathed in darkness, she couldn't see anything. She pressed her back even tighter against the hard, damp wall and looked toward the entrance. Whoever was coming would have to enter there.

A light appeared under the water, growing stronger as it neared. Suddenly a masked head and shoulders reared up out of the water, and then another. Scared and disoriented, she shielded her eyes from their spotlight.

"Marissa!" a voice called out, echoing oddly in the chamber. A figure swam over and pulled off his mask. Even after she recognized Spencer, she remained cowered in the corner, her hands in front of her face.

"Your brother's alive." Spencer spoke gently, as if explaining the end of a war to a six-year-old. "He's in the hospital. Steve and the others are being held for questioning." He reached for her hand, and a look of pain flashed through his eyes when she pulled away.

An EMT wearing full scuba gear approached. "Hypothermia," he said quietly to Spencer. "We can handle things now."

Spencer moved away as the technician slipped a mask over Marissa's face and eased her in the water. Halfway out, she panicked and attempted to rip the mask off, but strong arms held her and the next thing she felt was the gentle lifting of a helicopter.

Thirty-eight

*T*welve hours later Marissa woke up in the Wailuku hospital. "Good morning," a nurse said, smiling down as she took Marissa's pulse. "More liquids, a lot of rest, and you'll be as good as new. And if you promise to take care of yourself, you can go home today." Marissa's muscles ached as she gingerly moved her arms and legs. "A friend of yours stayed with you all night," the nurse said, turning to leave. "I'll let her back in."

A moment later Lynn was at the door. With tentative steps, she neared Marissa's bed. "John called and told me what happened. I couldn't believe it," Lynn began, her voice trembling. "I would have never agreed if I thought they would hurt you. They—" A tear ran down her face. "They said they wanted the money. I was so jealous of you that I thought if the place was robbed, you'd lose your job." Her lower lip trembled uncontrollably. "I just stayed here to make sure you were okay. I'll understand if you never speak to me again—if you want nothing to do with me." Lynn lowered her head and turned to leave.

"That's not how I like to treat a friend," Marissa said softly.

Lynn slowly turned, meeting Marissa's eyes reluctantly but with a glimmer of hope.

"You made a mistake, but I forgive you. Thank God the nightmare is over. But . . . did . . . did my brother make it?" Marissa held her breath waiting for the answer.

"Yes," Lynn said, her eyes brighter. "The nurses say he's

doing well. I know his room number. I'll take you there." She pushed a wheelchair over from across the room, insisting that Marissa ride.

"Here it is." Lynn escorted Marissa on what appeared to be a familiar route, as though she had been there many times before. After Lynn opened the door for her, she squeezed Marissa's hand and then discreetly slipped away.

"Michael," Marissa whispered, walking over to the still form in the bed. He was hooked up to several machines and he looked pale, but somehow knowing he was getting better made the weeks of frustration and struggle melt away.

His eyes opened and he stretched out his thin arm toward her. "I'm sorry," he whispered.

"That's all behind us now." Marissa took his hand and enveloped it within her own. "Thank God we're alive. As soon as you're well, we'll leave this island." Instead of a confirming nod, his eyes darted to the wall and then back to her again.

"There are others like me still there," Michael said. Marissa saw the anguish in his eyes, and a depth in him she hadn't seen before.

"Sorry to interrupt," a man's voice said from the doorway.

"Gabe," Michael said, smiling. "Marissa, this is Gabriel Hawkins. He kept me alive in that place."

Marissa swallowed hard. The older man's presence reminded her of her impatience and the failed escape. "Forgive me for—"

Gabriel shook his head. "Don't apologize," he said, his strong, wrinkled hand firmly grasping hers. "Shortly after I left your cell, Steve discovered my placebo for the drugs. God hid me long enough to escape on the boat I had arranged for you two. So you see, everything works for good for those who love the Lord."

"And Gabriel's network is still helping families get their loved ones back," Michael said. "They have a lawyer and everything." He paused, his eyes searching hers. "I want to stay here and help, too. We can hopefully expose them from the outside now. Especially with my testimony."

Marissa's first thought was no—she wanted Michael back home, safe—but she saw the desire in his eyes and thought back to her own grief. Who could better help than someone who had been through the ordeal?

"You have a wonderful friend," Michael said. "Spencer set his radio to a frequency signaling trouble—a hijacking. The police were waiting in ambush when we landed. He was worried sick about you and how you would survive the dive. But he knew if he acknowledged you in front of the others, we all would have been killed."

"Where is he?" Marissa suddenly felt infused with a renewed sense of energy.

"He said he had a resignation to turn in at the hotel and then some deliveries to make."

● ● ● ●

"Sugarcane runway," Marissa told the cab driver. "And hurry, please." She sat in the back of the cab praying Spencer would be there. When they turned off on the gravel road, a dust cloud hazed the area but not enough that she couldn't make out Spencer's helicopter. Handing the driver the fare, she climbed out and ran, waving her arms as if he were piloting her rescue chopper out of enemy territory.

"Spencer!" she yelled, even though she knew her voice would be stifled by the wind. Instead of continuing, the helicopter circled and then gently set down.

A moment later Spencer ducked under the rotors and walked toward her, a big grin on his face. "Believe me, I can't fly you all the way to Portland."

"I don't want to go back," she said, her shirt billowing and hair flitting around her face.

"Are you sure?"

Marissa nodded as a tear rolled down her face.

"Well," he said, gently brushing the tear away, "since you

already know how to swim, I think you're ready for some flying lessons."

"Only if I can be with you. I love you."

Laughing, crying, she kissed him, and when he lifted her off the ground and twirled her around, she raised her eyes and thanked God for life—overflowing, abundant life.